The Mystery of the Planet Alas-K

Layout: Van Troi Tran

Desktop graphic designer: Elisabeth Hellmer,
Druckerei Robitschek & Co Ges.m.b.H.
1050 Vienna, Schlossgasse 10-12, Austria.

Printed in Austria, in Canada and in the United States of America.
Printed by Wograndl Druck / Mattersburg / Austria / www.wograndl.com

The Mystery of the Planet Alas-K

How something unbearable came to the planet of the bears

Story by Tatjana Barazon

Drawings by Van Troi Tran

From Shanghai to Watertown to Paris to Québec to Vienna to Salzburg and back to Alas-K

Published by ©VVG 2018
ISBN 978-3-200-05646-6

ACKNOWLEDGMENTS

Merci, Troi, d'avoir donné l'inspiration à cette histoire avec ton amour des ours et tes dessins magnifiques.

Thank you, Steve, for providing the space and time for writing so much of this story at your house. And most of all, thank you for making the Kitchen Giraffe and the Knight of the Round Ear so happy.

Thank you, Deirdre, for being the toughest, most meticulous editor in the whole world.

Danke, mein Papi, für alle die Zeit, die Geduld, die Freude und das ganze Glück, das es nur gibt, weil es Dich gibt.

Hugh's toy store

Hugh opened his little toy store with a sigh.

Every morning, he unlocked the door, rolled out the sunshade outside the shop window, arranged the toys, dusted the floor and put on his apron. Then he sat down behind the counter and waited.

Hugh owned the only toy store in his small town, right between the Florist's and the Comic Book Store. But hardly anyone ever bought a toy from him. He sold wooden trains and dolls and plastic figurines. He also sold board games and jigsaw puzzles, but somehow the things he sold were all very dull and no one was ever really excited about anything that Hugh sold at his shop.

Hugh was liked by his fellow citizens and often people came by to chat with him about their day and their family life. He was a good neighbor and a friendly man, but he was the worst toy store owner in the whole world.

All day long, he watched people come and go outside his shop. He looked at the hustle and bustle on Main Street and tried to think of something that would make his business thrive.

Anouk stopped by then, interrupting his thoughts with her joyful greeting.

"Hello Hugh, how is business going today?"

"Oh, hello Anouk, same as yesterday, I am afraid." Hugh replied with a sigh. "Why don't you sit down and tell me about your day?"

Anouk sat down in a comfortable chair across from him and started telling Hugh about the bears.

"You know what, I know about a place where the most wonderful teddy bears exist. A planet for bears. Not live bears, not teddy bears, something in-between..."

When Hugh walked home that night, he had not sold much once again, but he felt happier and even had a little spring in his step. The most wonderful teddy bears! That was something to feel good about.

He opened the door to his home, and immediately his son Anton jumped into his arms.

"Daddy, Mommy is going to see the bears! Mommy is going to see the bears!"

"What bears? Slow down, tell me." Hugh sat Anton down on the sofa.

"She will tell you! Mom, Daddy is home, tell him about the bears!" Anton ran to the bedroom.

'*Only, if you can say it without hesitation...*'

Harriet was reading one of the Inuit newspapers from Alaska she had found at the library. She could read the native language Inuktitut and while she was browsing through bear-related articles in Alaska in preparation of her trip, she had discovered something amazing. This time it was not about real live bears, but about teddy bears who had surfaced mysteriously in the snow. Harriet wanted to keep this a secret. Perhaps she could bring some of those bears back home to Hugh and Anton.

"Mom!" Anton called again.

"Yes, my dear. Just a second."

Harriet stopped deciphering the Eskimo newspaper and put it quickly away in the folder with her secret papers.

"Yes, yes, I am coming," she said and went into the living room to greet her husband. She hugged him and whispered. "Hugh, it has finally come through. I can go!"

Hugh looked at Harriet and smiled at her with a hint of sadness.

"You are going to see the bears? That's fantastic. You have been waiting for so long. I am so happy for you!"

Hugh hugged Harriet tightly, and tried to hide his misgivings from her joy. She would leave, and he would not know how to be without her.

"Yes. The university has finally accepted my application! I can join the next expedition to Alaska to observe the grizzly bears, and if I am very lucky, I can go to the more remote areas and study my polar bears as well!"

Harriet had been trying to go on that bear expedition for more than three years now as part of her zoology program. She studied the behavior and the shape of both Alaskan brown bears and polar bears, and she was very eager to see them in their natural habitat.

"Mom is going to see the bears! Mom is going to see the bears!" Anton shouted, and jumped across the room.

"Bears. Again. And she will be gone."

His little sister Sophie had joined them in the living-room and had brought the blender from the kitchen. The stick blender was her favorite toy these days. Sophie was not quite as fond of bears as her brother was. "Are you going to see giraffes as well?" she asked.

Harriet lifted Sophie up and kissed her. "No, honey, there are no giraffes in Alaska."

"I knew it," she said with distinct disapproval.

"I won't be gone very long. And I will bring you all the best bears in the world!" Harriet hugged Sophie tightly.

"Always bears." Sophie was disappointed. "I want a giraffe. And an Appropriate Horse. And a Wood Hound. He is very famous."

"No, no, just bears!" Anton shouted. "Bring me a big brown bear with a pointy muzzle and round ears!"

"A real bear?" Harriet laughed.

"A real huge live bear, yes!"

Bears falling in the snow

Koonan moved slowly deeper and deeper into the forest.

"Hey, can we come closer now?" one of the hunters asked. The group had stayed behind. They were waiting for Koonan's signal to make further steps.

"Wait, stay back! I just heard something."

Koonan was an experienced young scout who knew every single sound of the forest. A deer raising its head, a rabbit running, a bird in flight; not even the slightest sound escaped Koonan's keen hearing. He had known the forest of Koonan all his life but he explored it anew every day.

He went around a tree, but then stopped dead in his tracks. He heard a sound that he had never heard before. As if something had fallen from very, very high above and landed in the snow right beside him, making almost no noise at all. Nothing but a muffled, soft, almost inaudible sound.

"Stay right where you are. I will go and see what it is."

He looked up. A little snow shook from the tree top of a tall black spruce tree. He followed the falling snow to the ground and there he saw a shape.

Koonan approached the tree very carefully making no sound himself. His body stretched forward and, with his legs bent, he put the tip of his spear into the ground. Something stirred. Koonan stepped closer. Snowflakes fell off a rounded ear in the snow. Koonan held his breath. He knelt down and removed some more snow from the small, soft-looking thing and uncovered a tiny brown bear that was made of a silky material. He shook the bear, but the bear didn't wake up. Koonan instinctively put the bear's muzzle to his cheek and rubbed it a few times.

All at once, Koonan's perception of the world became pure bliss. No stress or anxiety. Only joy. He stayed like this for a few moments wishing this wonder would never end.

"Hey, Koonan. What's going on?" The hunters had stayed behind, holding their breath and waiting to put their feet on the ground. Koonan was only a few steps ahead but had disappeared out of sight.

Koonan hugged the little soft bear, enjoying the blissfulness before he had to slip back into reality.

"No other animals than bears!"

The planet Alas-K is a planet where bears live. Only bears. Those bears are not like the ones that live on Earth. They are not teddy bears, and not live bears either, they are something in-between. They are created by wishes.

The bears who are in charge, like the President of the planet, Old Teddy Bear, the chief bear observer Little Creamy, or the journalist-philosopher Bearmouse and a few others, are former teddy bears who have been lost or abandoned by their child and have been brought to Alas-K by Nelson, Leader of the Abandoned Bears Rescue Squad. All other bears on the planet are spontaneous creations of wishes.

Only Faunour was not really one of them. He was a spontaneous bear creation, yes, but completely free, as no wish had created him. He was of the rarest teddy bear kind on Alas-K. He had come into existence out of nothing, out of the blue. As the pure negation of nothingness, Faunour had simply appeared on the planet one day. Bears like him were destined to bring about great changes, like revolutions or inventions.

On Alas-K, everything was about bears. There was a Bear Park for leisure, a Telescope Observation Park where most bears worked during most days, a television broadcasting studio where all programs were about bears, a school where the language of bears was taught, and a Nuzzling Studio and Workshop where the pink bear Adelaide was in charge of checking the appropriate shape of the bears. She was the appointed Nuzzling Supervisor. At the Nuzzle Training Center, led by the Knight of the Round Ear, the bears learned how to do their famous Nuzzle.

Yet Faunour often wondered why everything on the planet was only about bears.

What about other animals? Did they even exist? Where did they live? What did they look like?

Faunour's musings and curiosity about other animals came together to create an actual pathway to a secret hidden library.

Once he discovered the Secret Library, Faunour was amazed. There were so many books about so many things, places and animals he had never heard of before! He went there as often as he could, to take a break from feeling trapped in a world where only bears were tolerated. And he started to imagine a whole universe where all animals could live together. Faunour learned about giraffes and tigers and horses and dogs, and all kinds of other animals, too.

Sometimes Bearmouse would come with him to the Secret Library and they would read and dream together. As the journalist-philosopher of the planet, Bearmouse was very interested in new things. He discovered, looking at pictures from Siberia, that he was very fond of tigers. Faunour quickly turned the pages when he saw that Siberian tigers liked to feed on a particular kind of black grizzly bear called the Ussuri bear, so Bearmouse would not get frightened. However, he loved the fact that the Siberian tiger was called Amur Tiger, as it sounded like love.

Faunour and Bearmouse had now seen something that the other bears on their planet would never see, and they both wondered why everything on the planet was all about bears.

President Old Teddy Bear was very strict about the exclusive presence of bears on the planet. He also was aware of everything that happened on the planet and knew most secrets, even if nobody told him about them. He just knew.

When he started to sense the growing interest in other animals, he decided to call in all the bears for an emergency meeting to catch this danger in time, before it spread to the whole planet. The bears quickly left their posts at the telescopes to go to City Hall. General meetings were always an exciting moment, although the bears could not remember much about them once they were over. They had a very bad memory.

The bears had gathered in the big hall and exchanged glances. What was this all about? Had something happened?

Everyone was nervous and they stood close to one another, holding paws in anxious anticipation as to what Teddy Bear had to say.

President Teddy bear had climbed on stage and put his muzzle close to the microphone. His right eye was a little loose, and he had to adjust it repeatedly with the help of a monocle that he was holding in his paw.

"Hello, bears."

President Teddy Bear greeted them in a stern voice, after clearing his throat several times.

"Thank you for joining this public meeting. I have a very important matter that I would like to discuss with you all today."

He paused a little and looked around. The bears held their breath and waited.

"I have called you here because I need to remind you of the fact that this planet is the planet of bears."

The bears applauded and nodded.

"We need to study the bears on Earth very closely by watching them through our telescopes and observe the way they look and the way they walk and the way they move. How they are shaped and how they move dictates shape to our shape and this is how we can become the best teddy bears on Earth."

"But what about the wishes?" asked one particularly alert bear.

"Yes, the wishes are the fundamental incentive to our existence. They make us come alive, but in order to shape up as bears, we need to know what a bear looks like. We also need to remember what it is that bears eat: brown bears eat salmon they catch in rivers; polar bears eat seals they hunt on ice, and black bears eat bearberries and other kinds of small fruit."

The bears looked at each other and nodded. They wondered what this was all about. It was difficult for them to remember things, as the Alas-K bears had a moment-to-moment perception of things. Too much memory would have made them sad and heavy.

"Little Creamy is in charge of the telescopes. We all take shifts in watching the bears on Earth through our telescopes in the Telescope Park."

Teddy Bear paused and took a deep breath.

"But…!" He said in a louder tone.

Everyone was on the edge of their seats.

"It has come to my attention that a few among you are curious about other animals," Teddy Bear said. Then he paused again and waited for the reaction of the audience.

The bears in the audience remained silent. Most of them knew nothing about other animals. They didn't even know that they existed.

"Do I have your undivided attention?" President Teddy Bear asked.

The bears nodded, and waited.

"Not only are some of you interested in other animals, it has also been brought to my attention that some of you would be interested in having other animals on the bear planet!"

The bears gasped and held their breath, putting their paws on their muzzles.

"Does anyone have anything to say about that?"

Faunour looked at Bearmouse. Bearmouse nodded. Then he stood up.

"Squeak! Indeed, President Teddy Bear, I would like to speak."

"Please, Bearmouse. You have the floor."

"Thank you, President."

The bears started holding paws again. Other animals than bears? This was very exciting.

"Dear bears," said Bearmouse. "Our planet is above all the planet of bears of course, and we all know that and are very pleased with it. Bears are awesome."

The audience responded with an approving growl.

"But... you should all be aware of the fact that other animals exist. And they are awesome as well."

Some of the bears in the audience started protesting. Other animals were awesome, too?

"Where do these animals exist?" asked one little bear who was sitting next to Big Creamy.

Bearmouse looked at Faunour.

"They live on Earth, where Earth bears live as well. There are many other animals. Not just bears."

"Really? Is that so?" The bears were intrigued.

President Teddy Bear took the floor again.

"Here we have established a place where bears are safe. Don't you ever forget that. We don't want other animals on our planet, because they could threaten the bears' safety!"

"President Teddy Bear," said Bearmouse. "Please accept that other animals are equally wonderful. Especially tigers," he added, thinking of the pictures he had seen of tigers.

Faunour got up and stood next to Bearmouse, waiting for him to finish his sentence.

"Faunour would like to say a few words," Bearmouse told the audience, and handed Faunour the microphone.

"Thank you, Bearmouse," Faunour said and then turned to the audience.

"Dear bears, I want you all to know that there is a Secret Library in a secret place on our planet. It can only be found when you wish for it. If, by any chance, you should find the way to the library, you will discover books that show a wonderful variety of other animals. Tigers and zebras, giraffes, dogs and rabbits, and many other different kinds."

Listening to this, President Teddy Bear became quite angry.

"Enough! Faunour, I won't stand any more nonsense about other animals. This is the bear planet. If you are so eager to be with other animals, you should go to Earth. After all, that is the place where all animals live."

The bears in the audience held their breath. Teddy Bear was usually a mild-mannered bear and did not show any intense emotion, but this subject had obviously angered him.

"Silence!" Teddy Bear used his fist to demand that the bears be silent, although none of them even stirred.

Faunour looked at Bearmouse. And Bearmouse looked at Nelson. Faunour was not sure if this was a punishment or a blessing.

"Faunour will be sent to Earth and take care of our office in Alaska. We need someone to receive the bears when they arrive on Earth. Up until now, the bears have been falling to Earth at random. This will be the perfect job for you, Faunour."

"How will I know where they land?" Faunour asked.

"We will give you a map. You will have to find the bears and collect them and send them to the toy stores."

"Don't you think we should put this to a vote?" asked Bearmouse, fearful of losing his friend.

All the bears were in favor, and so it was decided that Faunour would be sent to Earth to open a little office where he would receive the teddy bears from the planet Alas-K.

"Wait!" said Nelson. "I don't think Faunour should go to Earth alone. I will go with him."

"Excellent," Old Teddy said. "Nelson, you know how to take care of things as the Leader of the Abandoned Bears Rescue Squad, and you know how to travel to Earth. However, this time it will be different. I need you both to be fully awake on Earth and not become teddy bears, and Nelson will stay with Faunour for a while."

Nelson had never stayed on Earth for longer periods of time, or without a Rescue Squad Mission.

"I will assist Faunour with everything." Nelson promised.

"We will have the office created by the Automatic Negation Activator," Teddy Bear continued. "And you will be all set once you arrive in Alaska. Robotbear will take you to Earth in his rocket ship. He can travel freely between worlds, as he does not have a sense of taste or smell he is not prone to transformation.

But before you go we need to make sure you have enough Magic Potions for your trip and for your stay on Earth."

The bears listened carefully to every word that Teddy Bear said. They nodded and then started mumbling to each other about what they just heard.

"Where is the Knight of the Round Ear?" called Old Teddy Bear. "He is in charge of the Magic Potions. Is he here? We need him to give both of you enough Magic Potions for your trip. There are many different kinds and for each new situation there has to be a new selection. Knight of the Round Ear?"

"Yes, President. I am here. *Clong!*"

Clong! was the sound that accompanied the Knight's every move. The visor of his helmet kept closing and obstructing his vision whenever he moved around.

"Here! I am here! Wait, am I here? I can't see you. Can you see me?"

While he tried to get up, the Knight stumbled over a few other bears who were sitting quite still in their little chairs.

"Hey, Knight, look where you're going."

"I am. I am. I am looking. But where am I going? And where is my Appropriate Horse, by the way? I have been looking for him for so long. Has anyone seen him?"

At some time or another at every general meeting the Knight of the Round Ear would ask about his Appropriate Horse. Most bears didn't know what he was talking about. Most bears didn't even know what a horse was.

"Alaska here I come!"

"Come on now, hurry."

"My suitcase is ready!"

Hugh rolled Harriet's suitcase from the bedroom to the door.

She was wearing her bright red parka and jumped around in the hallway.

"Alaska, here I come! I am going to see the bears! The bears!"

Harriet was so happy she could hardly contain herself, and so she forgot for a moment that her departure did not make everyone else quite as happy.

Anton was sitting in a corner. Sophie sat sobbing on the couch, clutching Tigah, the cat, with one hand and holding a funnel with the other.

"Oh, my dears. Don't be sad. I will be back very soon, and you will get the most wonderful bears, you will see!"

Harriet hugged her children. King Ademar was licking her snow boots.

"I hate bears," Sophie said, stubbornly. Her grip tightened around the blue funnel.

"Come on now, that's not true," Anton said. "Everybody loves bears. They are the best. Mom, you will say hi to the bears, won't you?"

"Oh, of course, my dear, I will make sure to hug each bear that I see and give them a kiss from you."

"A kiss? Now that would be dangerous, wouldn't it?"

"So maybe I'll just rub my nose on their nose?"

"A nuzzle?"

"Yes, the Nuzzle with the Muzzle."

They all cheered. And Harriet rubbed her nose on Sophie's cheek.

"Nuzzle with the Muzzle?"

And suddenly even Sophie smiled. "That's very sweet!"

"When you go to Alaska, will you please look out for a tiger?"

"Yes, Sophie. I will certainly do that."

"You know, Mom, they sometimes come over all the way from Siberia. They are good swimmers, you know."

"Yes they are, and tigers don't need visas."

Tigah jumped up from Sophie's lap, yawned, and in saying goodbye to Harriet, he rubbed his forehead on Harriet's leg.

"You see, Tigah knows the Nuzzle too."

Harriet said goodbye to her children, Anton and Sophie, Tigah, the cat, and not forgetting King Ademar, the dachshund of the family, who liked nothing more than blueberry pies.

"Come on, now, you have a plane to catch," called Hugh from the car.

They left for the airport where Harriet took off at last to the wondrous State of Alaska.

Bears and bears again

"Hey, Koonan! Wake up!"

One of the hunters approached Koonan, worried about his silence. Koonan had slipped into the snow and fallen asleep, hugging the soft bear in his arms.

"What is it?" asked Koonan, when Aklaq shook him.

"You fell asleep."

"Asleep?" Koonan sat up and realized that he didn't feel cold.

Koonan quickly put the little bear under his coat.

"What are you hiding, Koonan?"

"Nothing," he said, but a small round ear was showing beneath his collar.

"Oh, you have found one as well!"

"What do you mean? One as well?"

"Koonan, where have you been all week? Honon and Nita found two silky bears in the snow last week. They brought them to the meeting. There was even an article about them in the Gazette. A very strange phenomenon, never heard of before."

Koonan had been working on his canoe all week and had avoided everyone. He liked to be alone. Since his mother and father had disappeared, Koonan preferred his own company. The children had certainly talked about it, but Koonan had not been to school.

"Please, show us the bear!" asked Taqukak.

Koonan reluctantly took the little bear out from under his jacket.

"Awww, how cute!" Aklaq said, although he was a hunter feared for his ruthlessness. "He looks like a real live bear! And he is so soft. We have never seen soft miniature bears in these woods."

The boys had completely forgotten about their hunting. They all sat down in a circle in the snow and passed the little bear around. All Koonan wanted was to get the little bear back, but he decided to show them what he had discovered. He rubbed the bear on their cheeks and witnessed the blissful look on their faces.

Faunour and Nelson travel to Earth

Robotbear got the rocket ship ready for departure and checked that everything was in place. He had borrowed a huge screwdriver from Little Creamy who was in charge of the telescopes. The rocket giggled every time Robotbear fastened a screw. Robotbear understood how she felt and giggled with her. He made sure everything was ready to welcome the two bears being sent to Earth.

He put the box with the Magic Potions, carefully chosen by the Knight of the Round Ear, in the back and checked the seats and the seat belts. He also checked the coating of the rocket ship, needed for passing through parallel worlds. When they flew through the Imagination, a few possibilities could cling to the rocket's shell and make her swerve. The shell had to be perfectly smooth.

Faunour and Nelson were already seated comfortably in the rocket, and soon they were on their way. The rocket made a few approving sounds. Robotbear had left the screwdriver behind on the planet of the bears, so it was a little more difficult to understand her.

Faunour was silent. He was absorbed in deep thoughts about animals. Why had a planet of bears been created? Now that he was on his way to Earth, he started wondering why there even was a planet for bears only.

"Well, well, well, we are on our way to a big adventure, dear friends. Thanks to you we are the first Alas-K bears to go to Earth without turning into teddies. Well, at least I hope we won't ...," Nelson said.

"Don't worry. The Knight of the Round Ear has chosen an excellent selection of Magic Potions for you." Robotbear reassured them. "Use them sparingly and remember that when you take them it is always your intention that counts. The Magic Potions adapt to the situation at hand. They don't solve problems - they only help when you know what you want."

Both bears went into deep "mmhhh mhhh"- thinking mode for a moment and stared out of the cockpit window at the stars rushing past them.

"So, they are good for everything and nothing?" Faunour asked, after a while.

"Not exactly. In case you find yourselves in impossible situations, it will be good to have a vial at hand, but in general, it is better to manage without them. Just think of them as a last resort. Actually, you should take some now before we reach the Earth atmosphere. You don't want to turn into teddy bears, you need to rescue them instead," Robotbear said, after thinking for a moment.

Faunour looked at Nelson. "Go ahead, you open the case."

Nelson peeked inside the wooden case and saw bottles of many different colors. Blue, red, green, yellow. He took one out at random. "Remembering Alas-K"

"Oh, I believe we should not take too much of that one. Nostalgia is a terrible condition when you want to start a new life," Nelson said, already forgetting a little about their planet.

"True, but you mustn't forget the planet completely. We need to stay in touch. Nelson must go on his missions to save abandoned teddy bears, and Adelaide and the President will want to know how things are going," Robotbear said.

"Oh, you are right. The Nuzzle Workshop, and the Wish Captors. Yes, there are a few things I want to remember." Faunour rubbed his paw under his chin.

"Surviving on Earth for a few hours" was written on another label.

"What do you think? Will this one do?" Nelson held the bottle up to Faunour.

"Not so sure. Let me have a look."

Faunour climbed down from his seat and sat on the floor. He put his paw on the different bottles and looked at the labels. "Unmotivated move to Earth." "Passing through the Imagination unchanged." When he saw that one, his gaze met Nelson's. "The Imagination?"

"Yes, well, I don't know much about that. The wishes fly through there. I think that is where the ideas of bears emerge, among other things."

"Do you think we will need that one now?"

"Maybe not now, but some day someone might indeed need that one."

Robotbear was happy to escort Nelson and Faunour to Earth because from now on, children all over the world would receive the most wonderful teddy bears. He checked if he still had the list with the toy stores that Old Teddy Bear had given him.

"I am very happy that Teddy Bear has finally decided to open an office on Earth." Looking at the stars, Robotbear noticed that they were rapidly approaching Earth and so he said "Better hurry, you two, take a few drops of a Magic Potion if you don't want to turn into teddy bears."

Faunour and Nelson closed their eyes and they both decided to choose a bottle at random. They looked at each other and took a sip without looking at the label.

"We'll see what happens." They both thought at the same time.

...

"Welcome to planet Earth!" Robotbear switched off the engine and turned around. Faunour and Nelson were fast asleep in the back of the rocket. Although they were sleeping, they hadn't turned into teddy bears. Robotbear opened the door of the cockpit and stepped out. He stretched and looked around.

In a little distance from the landing spot, Robotbear could see a small square house with a flat roof. This had to be the house that had been created by the Automatic Negation Activator, he realized.

Creating something with your imagination creates it in another realm, just a split second away from here, so when the thing materializes there, it can use the time gap between the two moments. According to this logical property, a house was set up in the middle of the snow and Faunour and Nelson would be able to take care of the teddy bears from Alas-K once the rocket brought them.

Robotbear was very pleased and his shiny space suit glowed in the Alaskan sun.

"Faunour, Nelson, wake up! Look at your new home!" Robotbear called out to them.

"Come on, Nelson, look, there is our new house!" Faunour climbed out of the rocket, shook his ears in the manner of Old Teddy Bear, making a flapping sound, and jumped right into the snow. But quickly, he began to feel faint and slipped back to sleep.

"Faunour! Do you need a few drops of a Magic Potion?" Nelson called out, worried. He sprinkled a few drops of the potion on Faunour, one that would keep them alive on Earth. Robotbear turned around and shook his head.

"You will have to learn how to use them. We need you here!"

"Ah!" Faunour said, waking up. "Oh, I just had the most wonderful dream. A child took me in his arms and wanted to rub my nose against his cheek. But then you woke me up. What are we going to do now?"

"Let's go check out the new house."

"We should find a map there with the places where the last bears landed on Earth. If nobody finds them after three days, they evaporate into nothingness, you know. We have to find them fast! Also, I hope there is a list with the toy store owners' addresses all over the world who are waiting for our bears."

"I have the list," Robotbear said.

They entered the house. They were in a living room with screens and tables, there was another room for an office, two bedrooms and a kitchen. Minimalistic, but cozy. In the living-room they found a few paper boxes and wicker baskets. "Oh, those must be the baskets for collecting the bears," Nelson said.

"The bears!" Faunour just realized that he had been chosen by his planet to receive bears who became teddy bears as soon as they arrived on Earth. He went over to the baskets and examined them carefully. They seemed well suited to carry teddy bears. Faunour felt a little pang of sadness when he touched the baskets.

"So, my dear bears, I think this is it. I will have to go back to Alas-K and wait for the bears to prepare for their Earth landing. As soon as the Bear Shuttle System is in place, the first delivery will be ready. There is a Nuzzle Competition going on right now," Robotbear said as he left them to investigate their new home. "I will see you very soon!"

"You will be returning soon?" Faunour asked, to make sure.

"Yes, as soon as the Nuzzle Festival is over and the winners are chosen. Before I leave, I will do the Nuzzle with the Muzzle to both of you so you won't forget about it." And Robotbear turned around and rubbed his sleek metallic muzzle first on Faunour's cheek and then on Nelson's cheek. "Nuzzle. With. The. Muzzle."

And they both said "Ah, how sweet!"

However, in one blink of an eye, they had forgotten about the Nuzzle with the Muzzle and it would be a long time before they'd both be aware of it again.

Nelson looked at Faunour and Faunour looked at Nelson. They were now the first bears from Alas-K on Earth that had not turned into teddy bears upon arrival.

Getting settled in Alaska

"Harriet! Where are you?"

Eloise and Fred were looking for Harriet as they needed her signature to authorize her polar bear expedition on St. Lawrence Island.

"Here. I am here!" Harriet called.

She was sitting at her little desk. After unpacking she had set up the bed and put her personal things away. She had just started to take out the Inuit Gazette again to check on the teddy bears found in the snow, but decided to hide the paper quickly before anyone could see it. She didn't want her colleagues to discover her secret.

She had been so impatient to finally see Alaska. It was indeed beautiful, so wide and big, but also very cold and very lonely. She had her red parka and a bright green sleeping bag and yellow gloves, but she started to miss her home and her family.

Since they had reached Alaska, they all had been very busy observing beautiful bears catch salmon in the river close to their camp.

"Harriet, come here please. I need you to sign the form for the polar bear expedition." Eloise was the supervisor of their group.

"Another form? But we are here now. What do I need to fill out now? I think I have filled out a million forms already."

"Harriet! You wanted to see the polar bears, didn't you? Around here there are only grizzlies. If you want to watch polar bears, you need to join another research group. They are located on Chukchi Sea closer to Siberia. Perhaps you will even be able to study tigers while you are there."

Eloise stood in the entrance of the tent, waving the enrolment form in her hand.

"Oh, great. Thank you, Eloise." Harriet took the paper and sighed. "When are we leaving?"

"They are leaving next Sunday. But you can go on another trip. The shuttle comes by once a month. Our stay here will be three months, so you will have two more opportunities to go."

"Did you get some footage today?" Harriet asked Fred, the photographer.

"Oh yes, we saw a few magnificent specimens, but tomorrow should be better. We need to leave very early in the morning, if we want to see the whole group gather to catch salmon."

"Oh, I want to come too. I will stay here with you a little longer. Maybe I will see the polar bears next month then," Harriet said. "I need to prepare something now. I will join you later."

"OK, we will go and explore a little. See you later," and Fred and Eloise went outside with their photo equipment.

Harriet wanted to study polar bears very much, but she wanted to uncover the secret of the mysterious plush bears in the snow first.

She sat down at her desk and took out the Inuit newspaper. She went through the articles word by word and started drawing a map according to the indications in the text. The two lakes, the river, the hill, everything was clearly recognizable and Harriet thought she would be able to find her way easily. The article described very precisely where the little bears had landed. She put cross marks where the bears should be and realized that one of the bears had supposedly landed in the snow very close to where her camp was located.

Harriet wanted to find them and take them home to Hugh and Anton. Because Sophie didn't like bears so much, Harriet thought she would have to find a giraffe or a tiger for her instead.

When the map was ready, Harriet put on her snow boots and carefully looked outside. She didn't want the others to see her, or follow her.

In a little house in the middle of the snow

Since their arrival on Earth, Nelson and Faunour had barely started to familiarize themselves with their new surroundings. They had spent most of their time trying to find the right dosage for the Magic Potions, and they consequently slipped in and out of consciousness most days. Old Teddy and the Knight of the Round Ear had carefully chosen a few Magic Potions that would help the bears survive on Earth, but they had not explained how to use them. Or maybe, the bears had forgotten what they were told. Bears from Alas-K have a very poor memory.

"How many drops did you take today?" Nelson asked, holding the bottle up with his paw. He found that there was a lot missing already. And he didn't know what effect that could have on their existence on Earth.

"Mmmh," said Faunour. "I have no idea. I don't remember."

"Of course, you don't," replied Nelson. "They definitely should have given us written instructions. They know very well that we don't remember things."

"They must have forgotten that we have no memory. Ha Ha!" laughed Faunour.

"Come on, I think we should go out and explore. We don't even know where we are."

"Of course, we do. We are in Alaska. The place where many bears live on Earth. The place where our telescopes are focused. Close to the Bering Sea. On the other side, there is Siberia, Russia, where tigers live," Faunour explained.

He knew a lot of things about the geography of their location.

"Also, I must say I am not sure if it is very safe for us to go outside. We are, after all, live teddy bears and I am not sure that they even exist on Earth."

"You are right, of course, but I want to see what's outside. Aren't you curious? After all, you are the explorer! You wanted to discover other animals and bring them home," Nelson said, trying to provoke Faunour a little.

"Oh really? I wanted to do that? I have no recollection…"

"Oh my, Faunour, you certainly took far too much of the Magic Potion. Or maybe you didn't take enough? Or maybe you took the wrong one?"

Nelson put his head in his paws.

"I don't know, Old Teddy said, we had to remember our planet, that was one of the requirements to even come here."

"Really? I think I still have a very AlasKan memory. Well, I will take some more, if you say so."

Faunour began to feel confused and a little faint after taking all the Magic Potions.

"Careful! I am not sure about the dosage," Nelson said.

Too late, Faunour had already swallowed a few drops.

"Ahhh. Yesss," he said almost immediately. "I want the planet of the bears to welcome other animals. What a marvelous idea that is!"

Nelson was happy to have Faunour back the way he knew him.

"Come on, Nelson. Let's go outside and explore the area. Robotbear left clues as to where the bears landed. We need to make sure the bears will be found by us and not by somebody else."

Faunour took out the map that Robotbear had given them. The surrounding Forest of Koonan was represented schematically and they could make out a few x-marks indicating the places where the teddy bears were supposed to have landed on Earth. They had fallen from the planet through the Imagination and landed directly in the Alaskan snow.

The marks had different colors, according to the time of landing. Red for "approaching three days", fuchsia pink for "two days or less" and rose pink for "one day or more." However, all the colors had started to fade a little already.

Nelson and Faunour started out quickly on their way to the woods. Nelson brought one of the wicker baskets with him to collect any teddy bears they might find in the snow.

"Did you take the right amount of potion this time?"

"Yes, yes, stop worrying all the time about everything," Faunour growled. "The woods must be this way."

On the threshold of the little house, Faunour looked left and right, and he saw nothing but the woods and mostly, the snow. A lot of it.

"Oh Nelson, look! This wonderful white stuff. Oh, look there! Did you see it too? I saw something running. Or jumping? It was small and had long floppy ears. So, it wasn't a bear."

"A rabbit? Do they jump? Do they run?"

"Ah. You have read the books at the Secret Library as well!"

"Of course, I have."

"Let's go that way," Faunour said pointing east.

Three maps of the Koonan Woods

Koonan took out the map he had made of the forest. He wanted to find the silky bears before the others.

Now that the clan knew about them, he was worried that Honon and Nita would also look for more silky bears in the snow.

Koonan had marked the three places and they formed a triangle shape. The forest had two lakes in the shape of a teardrop. One that pointed to the west and one that pointed east on the other side of the hill. Those two lakes and the hill were the main landmarks for the woods.

Koonan has spent his whole life exploring these woods and he felt that everything was familiar to him, but the mysterious appearance of teddy bears in the snow had never happened before on his territory, and he needed to discover the origin of this new phenomenon.

Aware of every single sound as always, Koonan was hiding behind a tree because he had heard a noise.

...

"Shhh," Nelson said to Faunour who was still in awe about all the wonderful new things they could see around them. "Look, there is a young human. Right there. Straight ahead!"

"Oh, a young human you say? One of those who like the bears we send to Earth?"

"Yes, one of those. Look, he has a map, too."

Nelson, who was hiding behind a shrub, could see that Koonan's map looked strangely similar to the one they had. There were the three places marked with rose colored crosses indicating the positions of the teddy bears who had landed recently. And there were three more that needed to be rescued fast. If no one found them on time, they would evaporate into nothingness like all the others before them. The x-marks had started to fade already.

"We have to hurry, Faunour, otherwise our friends from the planet will disappear!"

"Nelson, I don't understand this. How come we have to collect teddy bears in the snow? I thought Robotbear was going to bring them to us in the rocket? This seems like a very unreliable system." Faunour was still having trouble adjusting.

"Yes, he will, but only starting now. Now that we are here he can do that. Before we arrived, the bears just fell down from the sky, landed in the snow and evaporated if they were not found. Like the bunnies. From now on, the bears will travel in a completely organized way. To be honest, I don't know how they managed before now. The children wished for teddy bears who came into existence

on the planet but were unable to go directly to them. Now
it will be marvelous! Children will get their bears!"

"I don't understand. Who took care of the bears before
that?"

Faunour began to realize that many teddy bears must
have evaporated before their arrival, and he became very
sad.

"I don't know, I think they just disappeared in the snow."
Nelson shrugged. "But please relax, we are here now and
we will take care of the bears."

"Oh, all right. If you say so. Because we should not let
our friends from the planet evaporate like that."

"Of course not, everything will be different now that we
are here. We need to hurry, look at the crosses on the map,
they are fading! We need to get there fast," Nelson pointed
toward the east.

"Let's go around the lake."

"And what about the young human?"

"Nelson! There is one! I think I see one! A rounded ear
sticking out of the snow!"

Nelson and Faunour carefully approached a little snow
pile.

Koonan was making circles meanwhile, just a few steps
away.

"Hurry, Nelson, the basket!" Faunour quickly collected
the little bear from the snow and slipped it under the lid of
the wicker basket. As soon as the bear was safe in the basket,

he closed his eyes and said with a faint, nearly inaudible voice "Nuzzle with the Muzzle" before he fell asleep.

"Did you see? Did you hear that?"

"Yes, the bear was awake. Oh, dear, we need to find the others fast!" As Nelson grabbed the basket, Koonan had heard the bears' paws touching the snow. Not even the slightest sound escaped his alert ears.

"Hey! Who are you? Stop right there!" Koonan whispered and came dangerously close to the shrub where Faunour and Nelson were hiding.

"We don't have a Magic Potion that will make us invisible, do we?" asked Faunour.

"I am afraid not," said Nelson.

At the same moment, Harriet had found her way to the same shrub in the same spot in the Koonan Forest. Harriet didn't know exactly how she had found this place, she vaguely remembered slipping down a snowy hill and feeling really dizzy. The research group had set up their observation equipment along the river. Eloise, Fred and the others were waiting for the bears to arrive and all eyes were focused on the spot where salmon were jumping out of the water.

Harriet had managed to steal away, when no one was paying attention to her.

The map she was holding seemed to have changed. One cross had disappeared and there were now two other ones that were beginning to fade. A strong wind blew up from the opposite direction making the snow fly about. Koonan lost track of his surroundings, and the snow-laden wind made him swirl as if under a spell. The same whirlwind carried the unconscious Harriet to Faunour and Nelson.

"Oh, look. A human woman! She seems asleep. How did she get here all of a sudden?"

"Faunour, it must have been the wind! A strange wind that brings strange things."

"Hello," said Faunour kneeling down to see her face. "Look, she has a pointy nose. And pretty rounded ears. And freckles on her nose, curly hair a little red, a little long for a bear."

If his memory had been a little better, he would have tried to do the Nuzzle. But as he didn't remember, he only lowered his nose to her face and came very close to her cheek. He put the tip of his nose to her cheek but stopped, as he couldn't remember the rest.

"But this is not a bear! This is a human woman!" Nelson cried out watching Faunour very closely. He seemed to be entranced by her.

"Yes, Nelson, of course she is. I know. But there is something very bearlike about her, I can tell."

"Faunour, what do you mean?"

"Nelson, give me a little bit of the Magic Potion that makes you forget! Quick!"

"But…"

"No but" Faunour was very determined and spoke like Old Teddy Bear. "We need to turn her into an Alas-K bear, otherwise she will tell everybody about us."

"Who is she going to tell? What does she even know?"

"Mmm, it seems to me that she knew about the bears in the snow. She found us, didn't she?"

"OK, if you say so. But we don't know the effects of the Magic Potion on humans. You are well aware of that, aren't you?"

"Yes, but it can't be very dangerous. A human must be much more resilient than a teddy bear."

"Honestly, I don't know. We are creations of these people after all."

"You see, that's what I am saying. They must be more powerful than we are, if they can create us."

Faunour took the Magic Potion bottle firmly from Nelson's paws, ready to sprinkle a few drops on Harriet's forehead. At the same moment Koonan regained consciousness and began to track the bears again.

Tracks of teddy bears in the beautiful forest of Koonan, that was something that he had never seen before.

"Quick," said Faunour "I hear the young human boy approaching! We need to transform her."

Faunour sprinkled a few drops on Harriet's nose. She crinkled it up a little as if she was going to sneeze, but in a split second she was transformed into a bear from the planet Alas-K. A very beautiful female bear.

"Oh, Nelson, look! A new bear!"

"And now what?"

"We put her in our basket, of course!"

And Faunour put Harriet in the basket with the other bear just a split second before Koonan appeared before them, pointing his spearhead towards the bears. Although it was not that sharp, it scared the bears a lot. They had never seen such a thing before.

"Hey! Who are you?" Koonan asked with a stern voice.

"Well…we…."

"Are you bears?"

"Yes…bears," Nelson said, shivering.

"And what do you have in this basket?" Koonan asked them, while trying to remove the cover with his spear. "Silky bears?" Koonan did not know what else to call them.

"Teddy bears you mean? Yes, there are two of them in this basket. Why?"

Faunour answered in his most gentle voice, hoping to put the child at ease. "What is your name?"

"I am Koonan, ruthless hunter of the Koonan forest."

"Oh. Did you hear that, Faunour? He has his own forest," Nelson said.

"Yes, very impressive indeed."

"But of course not, it is not *my* forest. Well, in a way it is, yes, but not like that. We just have the same name. By chance. Do you understand? And what about you? What are you doing here? In *my* forest?"

"To tell you the truth, my dear Koonan, we need to find two more of these silky bears quickly before they disappear. They fell down from the planet Alas-K and landed in the snow of your beautiful forest. We are Faunour and Nelson, two bears from the planet Alas-K, which is by the way the planet of bears, and we are very afraid of humans, and of live bears and of everything that is alive for real, you know. But we are most afraid of the bears, as we only know them from watching them through the telescopes on our planet. But we have never seen one up close yet. Do you understand?"

"Faunour, are you crazy? What is wrong with you? Why are you telling him all this?" Nelson whispered. He tried to shush Faunour, really worried about their safety now.

"Listen, Nelson, if we want to make it on Earth, we need an ally. And it is always good to tell the truth. This boy seems perfect. Look at his shiny black hair and his beautiful blue eyes, no one could resist him. And he has a pointy nose too!" Faunour whispered back.

Koonan bent forward a little and examined the two whispering bears. This was the moment he realized how strange it was. It must have been the wind, the wind sometimes caused very strange events, he thought and shook his head a little.

"An ally? And what's in it for me?" Koonan asked. He tried to appear tough but all he could think of was the silky bears and how he could get more of those that did the marvelous Nuzzle.

"Oh you, for example, you could connect the real live bears and the bears from planet Alas-K," Faunour suggested.

"Connect them to do what? What is this story about a planet Alas-K anyway? And what a funny name. You are in Alaska now, a region in the United States on Earth where many different kinds of bears live. Why is your planet named after our State?"

"But it is obvious, don't you see? It is like you and your forest. The planet Alas-K is called after Alaska on Earth because it is the planet of bears!"

Koonan had no idea how to respond to that and thought about it for a few moments. While Koonan was absorbed in his thoughts, Faunour checked on Harriet. He was impatient to take her back to their little house and wanted to wake her up. Koonan wondered why the name was the same as that of his forest. They had nothing in common, and what did the bears have to do with all that? He came to the conclusion that bears probably don't always make sense.

"All right. Let me see your map. I will help you find the other bears."

"Oh, thank you, Koonan. Here it is."

Faunour showed Koonan the map.

Koonan turned it in all directions before he finally said "Oh, ok, I know, we are here. We need to go that way."

Koonan had recognized the lakes in teardrop shape and the little hill. On Nelson and Faunour's map, Koonan could easily make out the shining x marks. He showed the two bears the way while Harriet's map slipped into the snow. One of her three crosses had now disappeared.

Adelaide's Nuzzle Workshop

Adelaide was about to clean up a little in her shop. The bears were about to start their Nuzzle practice and there were only a few touch-ups she had to make before preparing the competitors for the Nuzzle Competition. The Nuzzle Fest was approaching.

Adelaide took out the sketches showing the different steps of the Nuzzle and put them on stands around the room. The bears on the planet Alas-K had a very bad long term memory for images and emotions, but when it came to memorizing gestures they could remember a complete set of different positions in a row.

When the bears arrived, they happily greeted Adelaide. There were white bears and brown bears and grey bears. Bears had formed in all shapes and colors on the planet. And once their shape was stable enough they received a Wish Captor and then, when they were not watching the bears on Earth through their telescopes, they worked on their Nuzzle with the Muzzle proficiency at the Nuzzle

Workshop. Before competing at the Nuzzle Festival, their routine had to be perfect.

They entered and chose their seats, while Adelaide began explaining the classic set up of the Nuzzle with the Muzzle.

There was first the posture of the head. Where the bear had to look, to point his nose in order to choose the right spot to start the Nuzzle and how he should rub his muzzle on the child's cheek. Other things to consider were the different moods the child could be in, or if other people were involved in the routine, like other children or adults who could use the Nuzzle to comfort the child.

"The most natural position for the bear and his child to do the Nuzzle with the Muzzle is this."

Adelaide showed a drawing of a bear held by a child. The bear's muzzle was close to the child's cheek and he was about to be rubbed on it.

As the child was not present at the Nuzzle practice, one bear had to play the child and another bear had to be the bear.

Adelaide assigned the pairs.

"The larger bears should play the child as you need to hold your partner up."

The bears giggled and fell one on top of the other trying to lift each other up and to rub their muzzles on their partner's head.

"Hey, not like that. One has to lie down."

And another round of chaotic bears falling one on top of the other began.

"Oh my, oh my," Adelaide said after a while.

In order to explain the different poses that the bear could use when the child did the Nuzzle, they had to consider a few possible gestures. Adelaide explained:

"The bear can be grabbed by the neck, the ears, by both paws or even by the back. Each pose asks for a different approach. There is also the side of the cheek you need to consider. You can start the Nuzzle on the left or on the right. Oh, and yes, most importantly, you must choose the right spot."

The bears were fascinated.

"Here you can see the child holding his teddy bear by the neck."

"Oh, how can we do that?"

"Just try. You will figure it out."

And one bear started to grab a smaller bear and hugged him very tightly.

"Yes, that is a good start!" Adelaide laughed. "You mustn't forget to practice a lot, as the Nuzzle is done in many repetitions, as many that it takes to calm the child and make his worries go away. So, you need to work on your stamina."

The bears giggled. They looked at each other. One little bear stood up and started to wiggle his bottom.

"Stamina? Like this?"

"Well, little Wilbur, this is actually quite a good way to practice." Adelaide applauded. And she asked all the bears to do the same. They all got up and wiggled their behinds. Everybody found that really amusing.

When they had practiced enough wiggling, they sat down again, exhausted.

"Now let's see how the tip of the nose should be positioned." Adelaide showed the drawing with the child and the bear where the child did the nuzzle to another child.

"Sometimes you may be held up to the cheek of another child. Then you must be careful to keep your nose straight in order not to upset the surface of the skin."

Adelaide went to the bear in the first row and showed him how to do the nuzzle in a perfectly straight line.

"That's so sweet," he said and giggled. "You really are the Nuzzle master."

"Thank you, Karu." Adelaide blushed a little.

"The tip of your nose must not touch the skin directly as it might be made of a harder material like plastic. It is not always sewn with thread."

Adelaide held up a ball of yarn. "Remember when you become teddy bears, the material you are made of will change. You therefore need to be prepared for any Nuzzle emergency. When you have understood the basic requirements, please visit the Knight of the Round Ear to enroll in sustained daily training sessions until the Nuzzle Fest.

It is important to keep your effort steady so that preparations run smoothly."

The bears got busy practicing some more until they were exhausted.

Bears catching salmon

Koonan, Nelson and Faunour had continued their progress through the forest. All of a sudden, Nelson took Faunour's paw. "Look! Bears! Real bears!"

Indeed, while they were looking for the other teddy bears in the snow they had discovered by chance the spot where the grizzly bears catch salmon on the river. Koonan protected them with his extended arm and pointed to a shrub with delicious looking berries. "Go hide there."

Faunour looked at the berries and asked: "Do you think we can eat those?"

"Oh, are you hungry?" Nelson remarked. Then he turned to Koonan and asked: "Are these berries safe to eat?"

"Gooseberries yes, they are good for bears. Look over there, the bears are fishing!"

They both turned their heads to watch their Earth brothers whom they had only seen from very far away through their telescopes. They looked at them carefully with a lot of admiration but also with a little fear in the pit of their stomachs. The grizzlies were large and majestic, and they had big paws with big claws and rounded ears and a large head with a pointy muzzle. As all perfect bears do.

They sat there and stared at them for a while, when suddenly Nelson clutched Faunour's arm.

"Look!"

Nelson had noticed something that wasn't quite right in this peaceful scene. Among the many grizzly bears who were catching salmon in the river they saw two bears who were not real live Earth bears.

Yes, there were teddy bears catching salmon with the real grizzly bears as if it was the most natural thing in the world.

"Koonan? Are you seeing what we are seeing?" Faunour asked.

Quickly Koonan checked the whole scene in front of him. It took him a few seconds to notice the two intruders and he burst out laughing. "Oh my, those are our bears over there! And they are catching salmon with the real bears!"

"Amazing!"

"Puzzling!"

"Astonishing!"

The bears from the planet Alas-K who were supposed to be asleep in the snow had somehow found a way to imitate the real live bears and were standing on top of a few big rocks with their paws raised waiting for the next fish to jump.

"Oh, if only Bearmouse could be here to see this. This would make one fantastic presentation for his show "Bears are us"! Our telescopes never show this kind of thing!"

"Yes, we need to contact him immediately when we get home." Nelson approved.

Koonan approached the river slowly. He knew how to distract the grizzly bears so they wouldn't hurt the teddy bears. But as he was about to shoot his first arrow, he heard an excited voice screaming:

"Look, look, teddy bears fishing with real grizzlies. Come here, fast…, point the camera at them, this will be sensational news, the most exciting thing …"

Eloise had also spotted the teddy bears fishing with the real ones when she had stepped down to the riverbank to get some water. Fortunately, her group had not heard her and Koonan acted quickly. He covered her mouth with his handkerchief and dragged her towards the bush with Faunour and Nelson.

"She has seen the bears, too! What should we do?" Koonan kept a firm grip on Eloise when she tried to free herself.

"Let me go!" she yelled.

"Mhhh Hmmm," said Faunour in the face of this new complication. "Who is she? A friend of the other human, I suppose?"

"Quick! The Magic Potion!" Nelson, for lack of a better idea, sprinkled a few drops of the Magic Potion on Eloise's face.

They were staring at her, wondering what would happen, but Eloise did not turn into a bear, she just fell asleep.

"Ah, you see, as Robotbear said. The potion acts according to our wishes," Faunour said, happily noticing that his memory was improving, and that the potion seemed to adjust naturally to the situation.

"Koonan, can you please distract the big bears now?" Nelson begged.

"I will try. But apparently, there is a whole group of bear watchers. It really is a great spot to watch bears, isn't it?"

"Oh, yes, it is. An excellent location. Our telescopes on Alas-K are also focused on this exact spot to observe the bears," Faunour said.

"Wait here, I will try to distract them and get the teddy bears."

Koonan slowly approached the river once more, and this time he shot many arrows in quick succession directing them at the salmon jumping out of the water. He crossed the river by stepping on a few large rocks. For a split second, the fish froze in the air and the bears were also motionless with their paws raised, looking dumbfounded.

Time seemed to stop still while Koonan came closer to the two bears from the planet Alas-K and tried to snatch them away from the water.

"Hey! What are you doing? We are in the middle of something! We are trying to learn how to catch salmon. See, we almost got it. You stretch your muzzle out a little and wait until the fish jumps and then…

"Then you stretch out your paw. Like that," said the second bear. "Then you stare into the water a little just as you do when you do the Nuzzle. And then you bend your paw back a little in order to catch the fish. Just so."

While he was showing Koonan how to catch a fish he actually caught one with his little snout.

"Oh, my, look at me!"

Koonan was very impressed. "I see. That's great, but we really have to go now."

And he grabbed both bears and quickly made his way back to Faunour and Nelson who were waiting, muzzles agape.

The whole intervention had only lasted a few split seconds, and when it was over, the Earth bears woke as if from a spell. They shook their heads and slowly continued fishing. Something strange seemed to have happened, but when they saw nothing they resumed their normal routine.

A woman is not a bear

When Koonan reached the place where Faunour and Nelson were waiting for him, he held the two adventurous bears in his arms. They twisted and turned in his grip, as he handed them over to the teddy bears.

Nelson held the basket open and after they toppled inside, they quickly fell asleep.

"Oh my, oh my, what an adventure!" One of the little bears sighed before closing his eyes.

"Oh, wait, they caught a fish!" Koonan held the twitching salmon in his hand. "Are you hungry?"

"Well, Nelson, are we hungry?"

"Mmmh, we are getting there. Not really hungry yet. You should take the fish home with you to your clan. They will be happy you brought dinner."

"Oh, yes, you are right. I need to get back."

"Koonan, this was the most exciting day we have ever had," Nelson said. "We can never thank you enough. We could not have managed without you."

"It was a pleasure for me, too. I will help you find your way back. It is getting dark, but the bear watchers might still be around."

They had completely forgotten about Eloise lying in the snow.

"Oh, you go home, Koonan. We know how to get home, and we have completed our task for today, we have found the bears we needed to find. We will see you again very soon."

"OK, bears. If you are sure, I will leave you now. Goodbye."

And Koonan disappeared into the forest, with the bears' map still in his pocket.

...

Nelson and Faunour took the wicker basket with the four bears and slowly walked back to their little home.

"You see, everything went really well. We now have a human friend and we found all our bears in time."

"In time, yes. Did you notice what they do when they start disappearing?"

"You mean the fishing? Yes, that was very surprising. A good story for Bearmouse."

"Indeed, but I am most puzzled. How could they do that? They taught us that a bear from the planet Alas-K who arrives on Earth will vanish in the snow if not rescued in time. But we now know…They did not fall asleep, in fact they even started to imitate the real live bears."

"The bear from the planet Alas-K has an ounce of free will, you know that. So, even if we think we know what will happen, there is always an element of surprise, there is always something unpredictable, unknown that can happen."

"Yes, Faunour, you must be right. It is still most puzzling indeed."

"Yes, it is puzzling. We need to tell Big Creamy Bear about it. As the Secretary of Puzzlement, he will love to hear about this new development."

"Oh yes, all new puzzling things need to be written down in the Big Book of Puzzlement."

"Yes, yes, it is puzzling indeed, but it is also a little frightening. If the bears did not all fall asleep and vanish, who knows what else they were up to?"

"Well, I hope those were the first teddy bears who stayed awake and were able to such a daring thing as catching salmon in a river with real Earth bears. Perhaps it has something to do with our presence here? Now that we are watching over them, they might become bolder."

"That is possible," said Nelson, pondering over the question of bears waking and falling asleep, realizing that he was beginning to feel very tired himself.

"Oh, now we have to call President Old Teddy Bear. We have, after all, enchanted a human woman. This is something we need to report right away," Nelson said, remembering that he had promised to look after Faunour.

And they were still not thinking about Eloise.

"Yes, we need to wake her up. But we have to choose the Magic Potion carefully."

"And most of all we need to check the dosage," Nelson added, thinking that they were still having trouble finding the right amount of drops needed for survival on Earth.

And so, they ran along until they reached their square little house almost as white as snow.

Once they were inside, they carefully put the wicker basket with the bears down and went over to the screen connecting them to the planet Alas-K. In fact, they had not yet contacted Old Teddy Bear since they had arrived. They had been so busy.

Nelson sat down at the small table and tried to switch on the screen. Meanwhile, Faunour cautiously came closer to the wicker basket where the bears were sleeping and removed the blanket slowly and carefully, a little afraid of what he was about to discover. But the four bears were sleeping peacefully and he could hear soft sounds of "zzzz." He looked intently at the bear who had a distinct coppery color and whose eyelashes were a little longer than those of the other ones. He was spellbound.

"What a beautiful bear!"

Teddy Bear Emergency

"Hello! Planet Alas-K? Can you hear me?"

Nelson had put headphones on and was speaking into a microphone in front of the screen. There was a little bit of interplanetary white noise before the image stabilized. After a few moments, Teddy Bear became visible. He seemed very nervous and impatient to hear at last from his friends. He was flapping his ears and shaking his head.

"Hello, Nelson! What's up? How is everything? Tell me the news? How are the bears?"

Teddy Bear was jabbering, too many questions were popping up in his head all at once.

"Yes, President, everything is more or less under control," Nelson replied.

"What do you mean "more or less"?"

"Well, the house, the bears, the forest, are all fine. But the Magic Potions…"

"What about the Magic Potions?" Teddy Bear asked anxiously.

"We don't really know how to use them."

"Oh, we should have given you written instructions. We always forget that Alas-K bears have no memory."

"Yes, no memory indeed. But Robotbear told us that the Potions act the way we want them to."

In a flash, Nelson suddenly remembered Eloise who might still be at the same spot where they had left her.

"Teddy Bear! I have amazing news. We have found a human woman and we changed her into an Alas- K bear. She is asleep in the basket with the other bears." With one deep breath, he had delivered the whole message quickly so he wouldn't lose courage. Faunour looked at him, amazed.

"What? But why did you do that? It is dangerous to approach humans at all, and even more so to transform them. We don't know what the effects could be on their imagination long term, and therefore, on us, do you understand?"

Teddy Bear got very nervous and scared and started jabbering even more than usual. His monocle fell out of his loose eye a lot. He had not anticipated that the bears would be up to so much mischief the moment they arrived on Earth, even before they would start shipping bears to the toy stores.

"Mmmh hmmm, President, I see. What should we do now?"

"Oh, I think you should try and wake her."

"But she is sleeping so peacefully."

"Please do. Take the Magic Potion number 2. A few drops on the forehead, that should work."

"Number 2? Which one is that?"

"Number 2 is the Magic Potion that connects various states of being."

"But is she going to change into a human again? I would very much like for her to stay a bear." Faunour worried.

"You will have to try it out, we don't know how humans react to our potions. Try one drop, Faunour."

Faunour took the bottle filled with Magic Potion n°2 and very carefully placed one drop from the bottle with his paw on Harriet's forehead.

Harriet slowly opened her eyes and shook her head a little.

"Where am I? Who are you? Bears?"

Faunour and Nelson watched her very closely. Teddy Bear on the screen was holding his breath in anticipation. Harriet slowly turned into a woman again.

"Hello," Faunour said. "Beautiful bear woman, what's your name?"

"Bear woman? My name is…oh, I can't remember."

"President Teddy Bear, she doesn't remember her name!" Faunour cried out in alarm.

"Well, you need to give her another drop then," advised Teddy Bear from the screen.

Faunour took a second drop from the bottle and put his paw on her forehead.

Quickly, she said "Harriet! My name is Harriet! We need to tell Hugh and Anton and Sophie! And the people who watch the bears!"

"Tell them what?"said the bears all at the same time.

"About the plush bears in the snow." Harriet felt suddenly very faint again. She tried to focus on the surroundings, a cozy nicely lit room with two animated teddy bears who were talking to her. That had to be a dream! She shook her head again and her hair formed a beautiful golden curly cascade.

"Hugh! He needs bears," she said and fell asleep again.

"Teddy Bear, Nelson! I think she knows a toy store owner," Faunour said.

"Look at the list that I have given Robotbear for you. It must be on the desk. The names of the selected toy store owners are written on it," Teddy Bear said.

Nelson and Faunour dove towards the table in haste and quickly found the list. The first name was indeed Hugh's. It read "Toy store owner in great need of bears with rounded ears and a pointy muzzle beneath a flat forehead."

"Mmmh, Hugh. He is the first on our list. Is that the same one?"

"Yes, certainly. You need to call him up at once!"

"But what about Harriet? Can we keep her?" Faunour asked, his eyes lighting up with hope.

"You will have to discuss that with Hugh," Teddy Bear said. "I will go now so you can call him. I have left the contact information on the sheet. Good luck, dear bears.

At present we are preparing things for the Nuzzle Festival, the bears are getting ready for the competition. You two should be prepared to receive the rocket and its cargo of the most marvelous teddy bears within a few days. No more collecting them in the snow! I am so excited to know that the bears will finally reach the children who have wished for them."

"Yes, that is wonderful indeed! Thank you, President, until then."

Before Nelson ended the communication with the planet Alas-K he remembered that there was something puzzling he had forgotten to report.

"Wait, President, can you put Big Creamy on the line?"

"Why? Did something puzzling happen?"

"Oh yes, indeed."

President Teddy Bear called to the other end of the room where the secretaries were having a discussion. "Big Creamy, can you come over here please?"

Big Creamy was a big yellow bear called Big Creamy for his color. He kept the book of Puzzling Things and had to be informed of everything puzzling as soon as possible.

"Hello? What has happened? I am ready."

"Big Creamy, so good to see you. Please write down: Today we saw the little teddy bears we had to recover from the snow catching salmon with real live grizzly bears."

"What are you saying, Nelson? Is that right? That is so puzzling, indeed! Thank you so much for telling me. It will go into the book right away."

And Big Creamy went back to his desk to write the new information down in the Book of Astonishing Things.

Nelson smiled and switched off the screen. He wondered if he should have mentioned the woman who had turned into a bear among the puzzling things as well.

Keeping Harriet

Nelson turned around to Faunour. He was looking at the sleeping Harriet with admiration.

"Faunour, we have to call Hugh now!"

Faunour looked at Harriet again, then at the contact sheet and then at Nelson.

"But he will want her back," Faunour said in fear of losing his newly found friend.

"Would you like to keep her captive?"

"Well, maybe she will just decide to stay." Faunour rubbed his paw on his muzzle.

"Why would she leave her family to stay with us?"

"Maybe because she likes bears more than anything?" Faunour suggested. "We could offer an interesting deal. She stays here and Hugh gets the best bears. The winners of the Nuzzle Competition for example. That must be good for his business."

"Oh, Faunour!"

"Yes, and Anton will get you."

"What? Me?"

"Yes, you. You are the best teddy bear in the whole world anyway."

"Thank you, Faunour. But ..."

"No, no, no buts. We will call right now and see what he says."

Faunour took the sheet from Nelson's paws and dialed so fast that he had no time to feel afraid.

It rang a few times.

"Wait," Nelson said and interrupted the call with his big paw. "Let's think about this first."

"Nelson, it's genius! You will be the first teddy bear arriving at a human child's home according to his wishes. And Harriet could help me ship the teddy bears to all the toy stores all over the world. This job would be done far more quickly by a human instead of a little bear like me anyway," Faunour said, cocking his head to one side.

Nelson put his paw to his chin and started thinking again. "Mhh Hmmmm" He rubbed his paw on his rounded ear. Indeed, he thought that he would very much enjoy staying with Anton as his teddy bear. This possibility was far more appealing to him than staying in this house in the middle of a snowscape, while he waited for the arrival of his fellow bears from Alas-K. Then having to pack them up and ship them off all over the world.

"OK, if Hugh likes the deal, I am in. I will become a real teddy bear, too," Nelson said after a while. He looked at Faunour who was still admiring Harriet in her sleep. He had an expression on his face that was very similar to the one Bearmouse had when he first saw a tiger.

"But I will have to fall asleep as well, you know, Faunour. And we need to find the right dosage of the Magic Potions, and I need to find a way to be able to come back here. So many things to think about! I am on Earth also to keep an eye on you and help you out when you are in trouble. I am also the leader of the Abandoned Bears Rescue Squad. We rescue the bears who are lost or abandoned and bring them back to Alas-K. If something out of the ordinary happens, I would wake up at Anton's to take care of the emergency, and I would need a vehicle."

"We will have to ask for it, as we did for the house, and the telescopes and the rocket. It's good that we have the Automatic Negation Activator." But then Faunour realized something more depressing.

"You will be asleep, too? Like the teddy bears in the snow? But only temporarily, yes?"

"Well, if I become a real teddy bear, I would have to be asleep like all the others."

Faunour looked over to the basket and heard soft "zzzz"-sounds.

"Nelson, when they will be in their children's homes, will the bears still breathe?"

"No, no, they will be perfectly still."

"Perfectly still? But that's terrible," Faunour said, shocked to realize for the first time that the bears would not be alive anymore, once they became teddy bears.

"Once the Wish Captor is removed, the bear is only a toy," Nelson said.

"The Wish Captors? What are you talking about?"

"Look at them, under the fur of their tummies, there is a little box with stars."

"Really?" Faunour was unaware of that, he rushed over to the basket and patted one of the bears on their stomach. "You are right! There is a little box! And there are colored stars twinkling on it."

"Yes, Faunour, those are the wishes that have been caught. You have one yourself."

"I have one? But who wished for me? I thought I was a spontaneous creation that had nowhere to go. That was one of the reasons why I was sent to Earth instead of someone else."

"Yes, that's true. But you still have a Wish Captor. It is only empty for the time being. However, one day, you will see, wishes will form on your Wish Captor and you can go home, too."

"Really? You really think so? Someone will wish for me?"

"Yes, and it will be the most blissful moment in the universe. And all the happiness that can be experienced will be experienced right there. Just for now, you need to do this job."

"Oh, Nelson." Faunour was about to cry. "Let's focus on the bears and the right now, please."

"Wait, why don't we give Anton one of those bears," Nelson said.

"I guess we could. But I think he has wished for you to be his bear."

"Anton, I will bring you a bear," Harriet said in her sleep.

"See, what did I tell you, he wants a bear! It's perfect!"

"So, are we ready to call Hugh? What are we going to tell him? Harriet will want to talk to him as well? Oh, no!" Faunour was worried that his genius plan might not work.

"We'll see. Should we try to wake her first?"

"I am not sure. She might jeopardize the plan."

"The bears," she said in her sleep.

"You hear that? She only thinks about bears," Faunour said, pleased, and started to dial Hugh's number very fast again so he didn't feel scared.

The strangest deal

Anton jumped on the sofa and put his headset on. It was time for his favorite show.

"Something about bears, I am sure," Sophie said, climbing on the sofa next to him.

"Yes, indeed. Bears catching salmon. An excellent show." And Anton turned on the computer to watch the grizzly bears catching salmon in a river in Alaska. "Maybe we will see Mom."

"Oh, really?" Sophie came closer and looked at the bears with a little more interest.

The bears were raising their paws, with their muzzles turned towards the leaping fish, and every once in a while, one of the bears caught a huge fish in his mouth.

"Look, he caught one!" Sophie was happy and clapped her hands.

Hugh sat in his armchair and read the paper. Then he looked at his children and sighed. He took off his glasses to rub his eyes. He was a little worried about Harriet, as he had not heard from her in a few hours. Usually she sent text messages regularly. The last one announced that she was about to go and watch some bears.

Hugh also thought about his shop. From time to time a child would come in and buy something, but it was never with bright eyes or excitement. Oh, how happy he would be if only he could see the children excited about the toys he sold! The whole reason why he wanted to open a toy store in the first place was to make people happy. And what better job could there be than one where you made children happy? Now, he was seriously considering selling something else, something like auto parts, or houses, or books. Deep in thoughts on improving his business, Hugh was slowly drifting into sleep, when suddenly the phone rang.

The ring startled him and he jumped up. "Where? What? Anton …"

"Here you are, Daddy," Anton said and handed him his glasses that had slipped onto the chair.

"Now, where is the phone?"

The phone kept ringing.

"What if he is not home?" Faunour was getting very nervous.

Looking at the caller ID Hugh frowned, he could only see stars in a row. "Hello?"

"Hello? Am I speaking with Hugh?" Faunour said.

"Yes, I am Hugh. Who are you?"

"Well….mmm….this is Faunour calling."

"Faunour? What an unusual name. Are you French?"

"Oh no, I am not French, I come from the planet Alas-K."

"Alaska? But that's not a planet. It is a State."

Faunour had put the conversation on speakers so that Nelson could follow. Faunour shrugged.

"Alas-K. Pronounced like Alaska but not at all the same thing."

"Oh, OK, I understand. What is this about?"

Anton and Sophie turned towards their father. They had heard him say Alaska and expected to hear something about their mother or bears, or both.

"You see, dear Hugh. The matter is this."

"I am listening."

"We have your wife."

Hugh sat up in his armchair. "What do you mean you have my wife?"

"Harriet. She is here with us and she is a bear now."

Hugh shook his head. "What? You are not making any sense. Harriet is a bear?"

"Mom? A bear?" Anton was not sure if this was good news although anything involving bears was generally to be considered good news.

"Could you please explain a little more. How is it that you have Harriet? And why is she a bear and what does all this mean?"

"Well, you need to know a little more. I am a bear myself."

"You are a bear?"

"Yes, a bear from the planet Alas-K."

"The planet again. And what does this have to do with Harriet?"

"She likes bears."

"I know she does, but…" Hugh was now very confused.

"Let me explain. Harriet is needed here in Alaska. I need to keep her."

"Why do you need to keep her? On your planet?"

"No, no, in the State of Alaska. We are here now. Nelson, Harriet and me."

"Who is Nelson?"

"Nelson is my friend. He is also a bear. The most excellent bear in the universe by the way."

"What are you doing in Alaska?"

"We are in charge of the teddy bears arriving from the planet."

"The planet of bears?" Hugh remembered the conversation he had had with Anouk the other day.

"Yes, exactly."

"Why do you need Harriet?"

"She is going to send you teddy bears. The best ones. The most marvelous teddy bears in the whole world, but she needs to stay here with me."

"How is it that you have the best teddy bears in the whole world?"

"They come from our planet. It is very simple, really."

Hugh got up and walked around the room. The children stared at him but he made a sign he wanted to talk in private. He left the room and went to the bedroom with the phone.

"Please, Faunour, tell me again. Harriet will send me the best teddy bears? Are you sure?"

"Yes, starting next month the best teddy bears in the universe will arrive here and we will send them to toy stores all over the whole world, but you will get the priority. You will have the best ones. The winners of the Nuzzling Competition."

"The Nuzzling Competition, fascinating. Is Harriet OK with this? Can I talk to her? Will I see her again?"

"Well, right now she is in a very unstable condition, she slips from one state to the other, half human woman half bear. I think it is best to wait until we have found the right dosage of the Magic Potion before you talk to her. But if you agree to our deal, I am sure we can find a way for her to come home from time to time. You have a holiday called Christmas I think, and perhaps she could do the Christmas bear delivery on her own."

"Oh, how wonderful! So, she will be home for Christmas?" Hugh was relieved.

"Yes, but you shall promise never to reveal the secret of our planet and never to come here unless the bears change."

"OK, I will promise that. And what about Nelson?"

"Yes, I will send you Nelson and his vehicle, along with our contract and the manual of the planet Alas-K. Please remember that the special number that connects us should only be dialed in case of extreme emergency, do you hear? Extreme emergency! For no other purpose." Faunour insisted.

"Very well, we have an agreement, I will expect the bears to arrive soon."

"Yes, Nelson will be there in a few days. The other bears will follow."

"Thank you, Faunour. Goodbye now. And please take good care of Harriet."

" Goodbye, Hugh."

Hugh turned the phone off and rested for a moment on his bed.

In the living room, Anton and Sophie were still watching the bears catching salmon when suddenly Sophie said "Look, Ton, there's a woman lying in the snow by the river!"

Magic Potions and Decisions

"So, that went well," Faunour said, satisfied with the conversation with Hugh.

"Did he agree to everything?" Nelson asked.

"Yes, mostly. I think the element of surprise was a big factor in the success."

Harriet stirred a little in her sleep, her coppery curls covering half her face, her head tilting to one side and the other. "Oh, the bears!" she sighed. And then suddenly she sat up.

"Hello," Harriet said, waking up slowly. "What is going on here?"

"Harriet! How did you sleep?"

"Who are you?" Harriet asked and rubbed her eyes. "Are you bears?"

"Oh my, Nelson. She has forgotten about us already. Should we give her more potion?"

"Just let her wake up slowly. Give her a few moments to gather her senses."

Harriet sat fully up now and looked around.

"Where am I?"

"You are in Alaska."

"I know that. But this place? You? Who are you? Why am I here?"

"This place is our office. This is Nelson and I am Faunour. We are bears from the planet Alas-K and we are in charge of sending teddy bears to toy stores all over the world."

"Teddy bears! Yes, the teddy bears, I remember now. Did you find them in the snow?"

"Yes, we did."

"And why am I here?"

Faunour blushed in embarrassment. Harriet looked at him with her big blackberry eyes.

"You are here because I want you to stay with me." Faunour had decided to tell the truth. He reckoned that telling the truth was usually the best thing to do.

"But why?"

"Because you like bears."

"Yes, I do like bears. Very much." Harriet looked at the little bear. "But I like my children more. I want to go home."

"Yes, you like bears and I would like to offer you a job." Faunour tried to ignore the second part of her response.

"A job? But I need to return to the bear observation camp. They must be worried and wondering where I am. We are all alone here. The researchers from Fairbanks only come here once a week."

"Oh my, the woman in the snow." Nelson put one paw on his muzzle and interrupted their conversation as he remembered. "We need to go look for her."

"What woman?" Harriet asked.

"There was another woman who saw the bears too. We had to give her a little bit of the Magic Potion."

"But what happened? Did you leave her in the snow? It's freezing! Are you out of your mind?"

Harriet got very agitated and wanted to get up, however being far too tall for the small house she hit her head on the ceiling. This caused her to lose consciousness, and she became a bear again.

"Oh my, look Nelson, she has become a bear again," Faunour was delighted.

"Faunour, we need to take care of the woman in the snow."

"But what can we do? We are only teddy bears. We will be in great danger if we wake her up. She will jeopardize everything we have here and we can forget our plan to send the bears to children. The whole world will know about it."

"We need protection. We need the house to become invisible to intruders."

"Yes, let's call Teddy Bear again."

"No, we must manage this on our own. Let's use the Automatic Negation Activator."

Nelson concentrated very hard on the house becoming invisible until it was put in motion. When they looked outside they could see a slight flicker around the edges of their house.

"I think it worked," Nelson said. "What should we do now? Look for the woman or send me to Hugh and Anton?"

"And Sophie. But she doesn't like bears so much." Faunour added. "We must give you enough Magic Potion to turn you into a teddy bear but not so much that you will remain asleep permanently."

"What about my Wish Captor?" Nelson asked.

"But you don't have one, Nelson! You are one of the bears who occupy a key position on the planet. You are the Leader of the Abandoned Bears Squad. You used to be a teddy bear yourself."

"Oh yes, you are right. But I am still being wished for."

"Yes, you are an exclusive kind of teddy bear. You are Anton's bear. You don't need a Wish Captor. But you need to wake up in case of an emergency. How do we do that?"

"Maybe if I take a little vial of some Magic Potion with me."

"But where will you hide it?"

"In my car."

"But is it safe? They have a dog and a cat, and Sophie doesn't like things involving bears so they might not all be so welcoming."

"How do you know that?"

"About the dog and the cat? It was in the description of Hugh's household. The list that Robotbear left us is very detailed."

"Oh, I see. But I meant how do you know that they won't be welcoming?"

"I don't know. Maybe it will be all right after all."

"Yes, it will. Let's now create a wonderful car for you."

And they both concentrated very hard on the perfect vehicle with enough room for rescuing other bears around the world, and a hiding place for the little book and the Magic Potions only known to Nelson.

Eloise

Eloise woke up from a deep refreshing slumber. She opened her eyes and saw the beautiful Forest of Koonan. She rubbed her eyes, shook her head and looked around. Slowly her memory returned. She had gone to fetch water from the river and then she had seen grizzly bears catching salmon. Wait, she saw something else as well. But she didn't remember what it was.

She got up very slowly and removed the snow from her parka. The Forest seemed to be glowing all around her and there was a delightful sound. Also, she didn't feel cold at all, although there was snow everywhere. She walked a little in the direction of the river and looked for the grizzly bears. But there was nothing that stirred the water or the air. Only a warm glow as far as she could see.

She decided to walk back into the Forest and look for signs leading back to her campsite. However, she didn't recognize any landmarks that she had memorized previously. No teardrop shaped lake, just a river that seemed to stretch on forever. She walked a little more until she saw a sign. "Welcome to the Forest of the Same Name" and then she soon came to another sign "Famous Wood Pie Bakery, 1 ¾ mi."

Intrigued, she decided to walk to the bakery, it sounded perfect as she was very hungry indeed.

Following a path that took her over both hill and dale, she finally arrived at a little house with a sign above the door that read "Welcome to the Famous Woof Bakery. Come in and enjoy pies that allow travel to parallel worlds."

Woof Bakery? Parallel worlds? Eloise couldn't wait to meet the owner of this mysterious bakery and take notes. She approached the house cautiously, and peered inside a window.

Many beautiful pies rested on polished round tables set around the room. Little cards were placed in front of each pie, and Eloise tried to read them. She raised herself up a little on the window sill, but lost her balance and landed in the grass. Yes, there was no snow around the little cabin.

"Hello there," someone said behind her. "Looking to travel to a parallel world?"

In front of her stood a dachshund sporting an apron and wagging his tail that looked like a fir tree.

"Hello, Sir," Eloise said, blushing. "I am sorry, I have no idea where I am and what this place is. Are we in the Forest of Koonan?"

"Let us start with introductions. I am the Famous Wood Hound, and friends call me Ademar. I bake all kinds of delicious pies that allow travel through the Imagination. This is the Forest of the Same Name. And who are you, my dear?" Ademar asked, offering his paw to help her up.

She took it, relieved, but confused. "My name is Eloise. I am a bear watcher and journalist on planet Earth, I have come to Alaska to study grizzly bears. But now, I don't know where I am."

"Oh, that sounds like a pretty easy riddle to solve. Come inside, Eloise, and we will find the right pie for you. But first you must tell me all about the bears and how you came here."

Koonan meets Fred

On his way home, carefully holding the twitching fish in his arms, Koonan suddenly found himself face to face with Fred, the photographer from the bear watching group.

"Hey, stop! You! Can you please help me?" Fred seemed very distraught.

"Help you? What seems to be the problem?" Koonan asked, feeling tempted to throw the big salmon back into the river for it was twitching and twisting so much, and they still had a long way to get home.

"I lost my team mate. No, in fact I've lost two of my team mates. Eloise and Harriet. Have you seen two young women in these woods?"

"Young women? No, I am sorry," Koonan lied. "I have only seen bears today. And I must be moving along, you understand, this fish is very upset, and I must decide whether to eat it or to throw it back in the water."

"Oh, of course, please. I am just so worried. They have both vanished without a trace. And when I try to reach them on their phones it is like their number never existed."

"That is unfortunate. I am very sorry to hear that but I am afraid I can't help you."

"Would you instead help me find my way back to the camp? I seem to have lost my way."

"That I can do." And Koonan showed the way through the woods. Because Koonan was aware of any event that occurred in the woods, he had located the bear watchers' camp as soon as they arrived. Koonan kept an accurate virtual image of the forest in his mind at all times.

After he had brought Fred back to his camp, Koonan looked at the lake and he saw the shuttle boat coming over the water. On the deck, there was a majestic Polar bear raising his muzzle in the air. He was obviously looking for food, he looked slim. Koonan rubbed his eyes because he thought he was dreaming. Usually, polar bears did not come so close to the mainland. He looked at the bear once again before he ran off.

'Oh, how wonderful it would be if he could be my teddy bear', Koonan wished, took a deep breath and threw the fish back in the water.

Breakfast is ready

Anton poured milk on his cereal and Sophie tried to mix it with the blender. As usual, the children played with their food and waited for their father to come out of his room.

"Daddy, Daddy, what happened last night?" Anton asked.

"I had the strangest dream. Harriet was kept in Alaska by bears."

"But Daddy, that wasn't a dream! Somebody called and you talked about Alaska and mom and bears on the phone."

"Really, I did? I hoped that was a dream. I must have fallen asleep right after."

"Yes, and we saw a woman lying in the snow on an image taken by the camera that shows the bears in Alaska. We were afraid it was Mom!"

"A woman in the snow, really, can I see?" But when they tried to find the images again, she seemed to have disappeared.

"I have to go to work now. I will tell you all about it later. Tonight, Anouk is going to take care of you, I hope that's OK. I have to go to a town meeting."

"Anouk! Yes! She likes bears!"

"Yes, she does. I don't understand the whole fuss about bears all the time. I want a giraffe," Sophie said.

"But, Daddy, what about Mom?" Anton asked.

"She is fine, she is in Alaska."

"But I haven't heard from her."

"She is with the bears, don't worry, Tony. She will be back in no time." Hugh lied and sighed.

"She is being kept by bears. I knew it. Bears are bad," Sophie said. "They want to take my mommy from me. Good that I have the Kitchen Giraffe. She would never do a thing like that."

"What are you talking about, Sophie? Bears are the best. They would never keep Mom captive." And he started to push his little sister, getting furious.

"Calm down, Anton. Mom is with the bears, yes. And she will send us excellent teddy bears!"

At that same instant, there was a splash and a crack and a loud noise, sparks and stars. And then there was a wooden car in the middle of the room and inside of it sat the most wonderful teddy bear that they had ever seen.

"A bear! Mommy sent me a bear!" Anton cried out and ran to the car. He took the bear out and rubbed his muzzle on his cheek a few times. "Nuzzle with the Muzzle!"

"A bear in the middle of the living room. What else is new?" Sophie walked around the wooden vehicle and saw a book inside of it. "Daddy, there is a book inside the car."

"Oh, thank you, Sophie," said Hugh and quickly grabbed the booklet from the backseat and put it in his pocket.

"We need to go now. Hurry up! We will be late."

"Can I take my new bear to school?" Anton asked.

"His name is Nelson. And I think it is best to leave him here. You will come home to him tonight. He is a very large bear, and I don't think he should go to school with you. You are a big boy now."

"Yes, a big boy who likes bears." Sophie teased him.

Nelson discusses things with Tigah at his new home

When Hugh, Anton and Sophie had left for the day, Nelson slowly woke up. He realized that he was only a toy when they were around, and that he could move freely whenever he was alone. So, he got out of his vehicle and started walking around the house.

In the first room he found Tigah sleeping peacefully on Sophie's bed. Nelson jumped on the bed and looked closely at Tigah. When Tigah noticed something tickling his whiskers, he woke up. He shrieked when he saw the teddy bear sitting next to him on the bed.

"Hey! Who are you?"

"Hey, yourself. I am Nelson. Anton's bear."

"Oh, pleased to meet you, I am Tigah, the cat."

"Are you a true Bostonian?"

"Why?"

"Because they call you Tigah."

"Yes, indeed. That's how we say it here. Tigah."

Nelson smiled. "It is good to be here. Tell me, Tigah, what else is there to know?"

"What do you mean? There is King Ademar, you might want to meet him, too. He is a dachshund, a sausage dog, you know, the long short ones. I have no idea why he is a king, but he likes pies, mostly blueberry pies."

"That is so interesting," Nelson said.

"Is it?"

"Yes, I think he should bake pies for all travelers through parallel worlds. That would be very helpful."

"Oh, he would love that," Tigah said. "But tell me more about you. What do you do?"

"We, the bears, we do the Nuzzle with the Muzzle."

"And what is that?"

Nelson looked at Tigah from the left side, then he cocked his head to the right, then he came closer and then he rubbed his long soft muzzle on Tigah's cheek. Then he waited.

Tigah first closed his eyes, allowing the blissful state to wash over him for an instant before he opened his eyes and shook his head.

"This is your Nuzzle? The Nuzzle with the Muzzle?" Tigah got up and walked around on Sophie's bed. "No, this is unacceptable," he said after a while.

Nelson was astonished. "What is unacceptable? Didn't you like it? That is shocking!"

"No, no, it's not that. I loved it. But it is not your Nuzzle. It is not the bears' thing. We do that all the time. I would even say this is something like the cat's signature move." And Tigah started circling Nelson slowly, looking up his legs, then, without warning, he started rubbing his head strongly on Nelson's right leg.

Nelson giggled a little.

"Yes, this is nice. Tigah. It tickles a little. But it is not the same."

"Of course, it is. It is rubbing your face on another person's body."

"Yes, but look, Tigah, the Nuzzle with the Muzzle is performed on the face. Like this." And Nelson showed Tigah the Nuzzle once again.

"Meow," Tigah said. "I see. Like this you mean?" And Tigah started rubbing his nose on Nelson's cheek until Nelson said "This is very sweet."

"OK, I think I get it. But I am still not sure it is the bears' invention."

"We'll see about that. Let's go see Ademar now, sorry, King Ademar," Nelson said.

Do you know where teddy bears come from?

Instead of going to bed, Anton had his arms folded and was hiding in a corner. He was so upset he wanted to kick the wall with his fists and his feet, at the same time. Anton wanted his mother to come home.

"Do you know where teddy bears come from?" Anouk asked, softly.

"No," said the child, shaking his head stubbornly, a tear rolling down his cheek.

"They come from another planet, far, far away," she continued.

"Really? How far away?" The child asked, still angry.

"The planet of the teddy bears is a wish away."

"Is that very far?" The child tried to imagine the distance to a wish.

"If you believe in it with all your heart, it is not that far."

Anton tried believing in something with all his heart and suddenly felt a little more relaxed. He started to imagine a planet with teddy bears.

"A planet with teddy bears? What is the planet called?"

"Alas-K."

"Like our Alaska, where the bears live?"

"Yes, it's spelled differently. Alas-K. But pronounced the same way."

"Why is it spelled with just a K in the end?"

"Because it is one of many Alas planets. Bunnies have their own planet, too."

"Why can't they all live on the same planet?"

"We will find out about that. But for now, let's concentrate on the bears. On Alas-K, the bears are created by wishes that children send to the planet."

"So if I wish for a bear, it will create one on the planet of the bears?"

"Exactly."

Anton suddenly turned around and wiped the tear from his cheek.

"How does that work?"

"The bears on the planet catch your wishes with their Wish Captors."

"And what do the Wish Captors look like?"

"They are little screens with stars on them."

"What are the stars for?" Anton asked, having almost completely forgotten the reason why he had been so angry.

"The stars catch wishes, and their color changes with every wish they catch. The wishes come to the Wish Captor as color patches."

"And how do the bears come here then?"

"When there are enough wishes that come together, they create a fully formed bear and then a rocket brings the bears to Earth and they are shipped to children all over the world."

Anton took a deep breath. Wish Captors. He had never heard of that before.

"And what kind of wish do they catch?"

"You will find out if you tell me what things you wish for in a teddy bear."

"Well…" The child hesitated and put his finger on his nose. "I know. A pointy muzzle!"

"Very good. And what else?"

"And rounded ears!"

"Excellent. Something else?"

"Big paws. And a soft, cuddly body!"

"These are exactly the features that the Wish Captor catches. Especially the pointy nose and the rounded ears - the most important qualities of a bear." She gave Anton a big hug and all his anger evaporated in that same instant. He giggled and grabbed his bear. "But the nose must be soft too."

"Soft and pointy. Exactly. In order to do the most important thing there is."

"And what is that?"

"The Nuzzle with the Muzzle. It makes every child forget about their worries, everything their parents do that they don't understand, and everything that makes them sad. The Nuzzle with the Muzzle makes pain go away and leaves only pure happiness."

"And how does that work?" Anton was intrigued.

"Give me your bear and I will show you."

Anton reached for the bear he had tucked under his arm. Nelson had a pointy nose and rounded ears, a soft and cuddly body, padded paws and a big white spot in the middle of his tummy.

"Did my bear come from the planet of the bears, too?" The child wanted to know before letting go.

"Of course, and you can tell by his perfect bear shape!"

The child smiled and handed her the bear with both hands.

"Now, your bear will do "The Nuzzle with the Muzzle." Are you ready?"

The child nodded eagerly.

"But first, you must get under the covers. It is done best when you are comfortable in your bed and the bear can sit on your chest."

The child climbed into bed, and she straightened the sheets around him. She put the bear on the child's chest, and the bear jumped into place.

"You see, first the bear jumps on your chest, like that. And then he looks very closely at you in order to find out what you need, what you are worried about, so as to define the perfect place where to put his nose, just so."

The child giggled when the bear took a close look at his face, up and down, searching for the right spot to start "The Nuzzle with the Muzzle."

"You must know that at any given moment there is the perfect spot on your cheek to start the Nuzzle with the Muzzle, and only the bear knows where it is. This is how he can make all your worries go away."

Anton smiled and closed his eyes.

"Mmm Hmmm," said the bear before choosing the perfect spot on the child's face to start rubbing its nose.

And then the bear did the Nuzzle with the Muzzle a few times in a row, rubbing its nose on the child's cheek, gently and firmly, until Anton closed his eyes and allowed the infinite happiness to lull him to sleep, taking the bear in his arms and hugging it tightly.

Anouk kissed Anton on the forehead and left the room, closing the door behind her very carefully.

Tigah and Ademar

Next to the bed, Tigah had been listening to their conversation.

Tigah put his extremely soft paws tentatively on the child's bed.

"Nuzzle with the Muzzle?" he thought to himself. "What are they talking about?"

He jumped onto the bed, put one paw in front of the other and circled Anton's sleeping body carefully. Tigah came close to the child's face and purred. He started rubbing his forehead on the child's cheek, and in his sleep Anton murmured "Nuzzle with the Muzzle. That's what bears do."

"Bears?" Tigah stopped. "But this is what we do! We, the cats!"

And Tigah looked closely at the Teddy Bear that Anton hugged tightly. Did Nelson just wink at him?

Tigah shook his left front paw and curled up at the foot of the bed. "Nuzzle with the Muzzle! Ha! We'll see about that." He put his head on the edge of the bed, closed his eyes and started dreaming …of blueberry pies.

King Ademar had been listening and barked a little. He was too short to jump on the bed, and he didn't want to wake Anton. Tigah first opened one eye then the other.

"Hey, Ademar. What is going on?"

"Tigah, I have to leave."

"Where are you going? Baking pies?" Tigah joked.

"Exactly. I have to bake more pies."

"OK. Nelson wanted to talk to you about the Nuzzle. But he can't now, because Anton is here and so he has to be a Teddy Bear."

"I see. I will meet him some other time. Farewell, Tigah."

And Ademar disappeared on a path of stars.

Alas-K bears come to Alaska

Once they had arrived safely on the landing spot behind Faunour's office in Alaska on Earth, Robotbear turned the engine off and slowly opened the door of the cockpit. The rocket with the winners of the latest Nuzzle Competition had traveled through the parallel worlds and through the whole Imagination from planet Alas-K to planet Earth.

"Hey, Faunour!" Robotbear greeted him on his way in. He wiped the snow from his boots on the mat.

"Well, hello Robotbear. You are early. Are the bears asleep yet?"

"Getting there. I just checked and they were all cuddling up against each other."

"Let's go get them."

In the trunk of the rocket the bears were half asleep, still conscious of the landing but already quite dizzy. When Alas-K bears reach the Earth atmosphere they slowly fall into a dreamy, sleepy state before they turn into teddy bears.

Faunour and Robotbear went back to the rocket. The rocket made a few greeting sounds and let a light slide on her side.

"Hey, Rocket. Thank you for bringing the bears," said Faunour.

The rocket blinked a little in return. Then opened her trunk.

Faunour looked at the Alas-K bears with their Wish Captors. They were all sleeping peacefully, and after their Wish Captors were removed, Faunour knew their breathing would cease.

With a sigh, he took the box out of the trunk.

Harriet was standing by the door. The house had stretched a little to accommodate her human size.

Shortly before they fall asleep, the Alas-K bears remember their ounce of free will. A tiny remaining portion of free will. This makes it possible for them to change states and to become the teddy bear of a child.

"Do you want to come inside for some hot chocolate, Robotbear?"

"Hot chocolate? Faunour, you know very well that we don't eat or drink. Robotbears are immune to the effects of the Earth atmosphere on bears because we don't know about taste. And this is how we don't turn into teddy bears."

"Well, alright, it is just so cold here. And hot chocolate is so good," Faunour said with a smile.

"Hoimsli!"

"Hoimsli?"

"Yes, you know. The word for supremely tasty."

"You must remove those Wish Captors from the bears now and send the bears off to the children. They will be waiting impatiently for their teddy bears. There was a rush at the Nuzzle Competition this month."

"Yes, we have Christmas coming up. A big season for bears on Earth."

"Of course, Christmas. Many bears are sold this time of year. Well, so long, Faunour. See you next month."

" Goodbye, Robotbear. Have a safe flight."

"Thank you."

And Robotbear climbed back into the rocket. The rocket made a few friendly sounds and blinked before they took off.

Soon they were on their way back to the bear planet.

Faunour gets the bear blues

Faunour lifted the teddy bear box up and put it under his arm. Before he went inside, he stopped for a few minutes on the doorstep, and then, as he began to cross the threshold of his house, one of the bears winked at him before he went back to sleep. Faunour sighed heavily.

"Poor bears." Faunour sighed deeply once more, thinking that Harriet would leave for Christmas. If she left to return to her family, there would be no guarantee that she would return to him.

He entered the office and tipped all the teddy bears out of the box on to a large table. The teddy bears were now all asleep and Faunour put his ear close to them and listened for breathing. He didn't hear anything. He looked closely at them. They seemed perfectly still, so it was safe to remove the Wish Captors.

"I will be back, Faunour. Don't worry," Harriet said.

"Will you? Why?"

"I like it here with you. The parallel worlds are always open. Let's remove the Wish Captors now."

One by one, they removed the little Wish Captor boxes from the bears' bellies. The Wish Captors were all full of wishes that had come together to create those perfect little teddy bears. Children from all over the world had sent their wishes for teddy bears through the Imagination and they had all gathered on these fixtures.

Faunour sighed heavily once again. One of the bears was softer and rounder and had a pointier muzzle than the others. That one had to be the winner of the Nuzzle Competition.

"This one must go to Hugh. He is so soft and cuddly," Harriet said.

"Yes, your husband will be blessed. The best bear that won the Nuzzle Competition will make the children so happy. A Christmas sensation!"

"Listen, Faunour, I will be back with Robotbear right after New Year's Eve. Please don't worry," Harriet brushed over Faunour's belly with a soft touch.

Faunour had forgotten that he himself still had his Wish Captor attached to his tummy as he had never been chosen to be a child's teddy bear.

Anton talks to Harriet

"Mommy?"

"Yes, my sweet," said Harriet. "It's me."

She had managed to wake up really early and to stay a woman long enough to call up her son. She had sensed that he felt very abandoned and she wanted to reassure him.

"Anton!"

"Mommy! Where are you? When are you coming home?" Anton asked anxiously, hugging Nelson.

"In Alaska, my dear, you know that. I have to take care of the bears here."

"Yes, we have received beautiful bears for the store! And Daddy is much happier now. And Anouk helps him in the store now and she comes to visit us a lot and looks after us, too."

Harriet felt a pang of sadness. "Oh, that's wonderful! It's good that Daddy has help. There must be so much to do now."

"Yes, all the children from all the surrounding towns come to Daddy's shop. He has the most beautiful bears in the world, people say. There even was something about it in the Watertown Tab."

"Oh, that is wonderful news. I am calling to say that I will be home for Christmas, my sweet. We just have received a new delivery from the planet of bears. The Christmas bears are supposed to be especially wonderful."

"Really? You will be home for Christmas. Mommy! I love you. I am so glad. I have to tell Sophie."

"Yes, I will see you all very soon."

Giraffes don't have stripes

Anton played with his wooden train. Sophie was trying to put a little dinosaur in her mouth.

"Sophie, stop that! Don't eat dinosaurs, they become giraffes in your mouth."

"Nonsense. I am hungry. What's for dinner?"

At that moment, they could hear Anouk call them.

"Dinner is almost ready! Sophie! Anton! Come here please, I can't find the blender, I need it for the mashed potatoes!"

"The Kitchen Giraffe? Oh, I know where she is!" called Sophie. "I brought her to my room to play. She likes the Famous Wood Hound and the Appropriate Horse. Look!"

And they all went to discover on the floor of the child's room the stick blender painted in black and white stripes, big eyes with long lashes, wearing a blue funnel on its head, together with a small plastic horse and the dog, King Ademar, who looked rather embarrassed, turning his head towards his tail, where Sophie had attached a paper tree.

"Sophie, your imagination, really, I mean, you need to be careful with those things, there is a sharp blade underneath" Anouk laughed as she picked up the stick blender from the floor. Her hands stuck to the paint. "You painted the blender…"

"Yes, it is a giraffe!"

"But, Sophie, giraffes have patches, not stripes," Anton said, proud of knowing so much.

Sophie blushed. "Oh, yes…you are right." She put her hands on her mouth.

"Ha ha! You mixed up giraffes and zebras!" Anton teased her.

"No! You are wrong," she said and pushed him a little.

Anouk removed the paper tree from the dog's tail and patted his head. King Ademar wagged his tail with relief.

"Come on, guys, I just need to finish the mashed potatoes, then we can eat. Go wash up. Me too, by the way," she said, looking at the black and white stripes on her hands.

Anouk went back to the kitchen.

Anton looked at Sophie with his blackberry eyes.

"Why is it an Appropriate Horse?"

"Well, Anton, that is perfectly obvious. The bear says that."

"What bear?"

"The Knight of the Round Ear. He is looking for his horse. But the bears are at Faunour's now. They need to be saved."

"Sophie! Anton! Dinner is ready now!"

King Ademar shook his tail a little more. And they all ran to the kitchen table where roast chicken was served. Sophie's favorite. The mashed potatoes were particularly appropriate too.

"Mmmm. Hoimsli. The Kitchen Giraffe did some excellent work!" Sophie said and everybody laughed.

"Blueberry or lemon?"

There was a sudden spark, and Tigah stretched his paws.

"Where am I?" he wondered, slowly recovering his senses. "Oh yes, I know, I need some pie to get to the bears. Nuzzle with the Muzzle? Ha! This is what cats do."

"Welcome, Tigah," the Famous Wood Hound said, coming out from behind the counter of his Wood Pie Bakery. "What can I do for you?"

"Famous Wood Hound, good to see you. Your pies allow travel through parallel worlds, don't they?"

"Yes, they do. Where would you like to go?"

The Famous Wood Hound put on an apron and started circling the pie stands. "I bake many different pies, you know, and they all do different things," he said, pointing to the pies of various shapes and colors.

"Oh, I see. I would like to go see a bear. Faunour, to be precise."

"Faunour? He is the bear responsible for sending the teddy bears who arrive from Alas-K to the children. Why would you like to see him?" the Famous Wood Hound asked.

"He spreads the ridiculous idea that bears invented the Nuzzle, although it should be perfectly obvious to everyone that it was in fact the cats."

"What are you talking about, Tigah? Bears, and most precisely President Teddy Bear and Faufur on the planet Alas-K invented the Nuzzle with the Muzzle. Faunour, on the other hand, is not even fully aware of the importance of the famous Nuzzle. He was sent to Earth long before the bears discovered its secret power."

"Oh, I see. But we have discovered it first! The cats invented the famous Nuzzle. And the bears must know the truth."

"Well, you will need a very special kind of pie for this endeavor. Just walk through the store and look around, perhaps you will pick out the right one."

The Famous Wood Hound climbed on his chair and waited for Tigah to circle the room. The pie stands were sparkling with pies of many different kinds. Tigah looked closely at the strawberry pie, but then turned his head to the lemon pie, then the pumpkin pie, then the apple pie, and then he got dizzy.

"Famous Wood Hound, you have so many pies. How can I choose the right one?" Tigah asked, a little discouraged, and overwhelmed with all the choices.

"Get closer to the pies and close your eyes. The right pie will choose you," said the Famous Wood Hound with a confident blink.

Tigah frowned. 'Nonsense. How can a pie choose me?' he wondered. Then he purred at the blueberry pie, remembering a dream involving one. And indeed, the blueberry pie jumped into his paw right away.

"Jolly good! The right pie found you!" The Famous Wood Hound was pleased with the special quality of his pies. "Go ahead, Tigah, have a piece. It will take you straight to Faunour."

The Wood Hound watched Tigah eat the pie and saw his eyes light up with pleasure.

"Mmmm, this is the most delicious pie I have ever had! Thank you, Famous Wood Hound. Now I can go tell the bears…"

"If you want my advice, just let them believe it was their invention. It might be better for the harmony in the parallel worlds," the Wood Hound said, but then he thought, that if the parallel worlds indeed became disrupted, they might need him to bake more pies, which would be good for business. And he shook his fir tree tail.

"But…." Tigah started.

"Whatever you decide, Tigah, do whatever you think is best. I wish you good luck on your journey."

And the moment he had pronounced these words, four stars lit up in front of Tigah. He put his paws on them and was on his way.

"So long, Famous Wood Hound, see you sooon..."

The words stretched into the void created by the path of stars that led Tigah out of the bakery, out of the wood and straight to a very special place in Alaska on Earth.

When Nanuk first finds Faunour

Nanuk was playing in the deep snow in the Alaskan winter. Nanuk was a polar bear and he had come to the village Kaktovik on Barter Island to share the food of the Native Alaskans after their whale hunting season. Usually, he would go back to the pack ice on the sea and hunt for seals afterwards, but the raise in temperature on Earth had made it difficult for him, and he had chosen to explore other places.

Now the ice was melting and seals had become rare, having no place to hide. So Nanuk was hungry and had lost weight. He had decided to swim to the mainland, hoping to find other things to eat.

Nanuk wandered about in the snow and put his muzzle down to the ground to stir it up from time to time, hoping he would find something interesting.

When a magical breeze came up and the snow blew around in little fuzzy flakes all over the field where Nanuk was playing, he couldn't make out anything for a while. He just stood still and closed his eyes.

When the wind subsided, Nanuk was able to see a little house right in front of him. He lifted his muzzle up in the air and tried to smell something before he decided to approach it. He sucked the air in very carefully and thought he could smell bears, but not the kind he was accustomed to.

Slowly, he walked up to the house and circled it for a while from what he thought was a safe distance. He could hear a noise although it was not very loud. It sounded like someone was working very intently on something. Nanuk put his muzzle close to the window and sniffed.

Faunour was removing the Wish Captors that Adelaide had inserted in the bears. She was expecting to receive the Wish Captors with the next rocket so she could install them on the new bears who formed on Alas-K.

After each Wish Captor removal, Faunour sighed with sorrow but then, he had a brainwave. The Wish Captor could be catching wishes for other animals!

Usually, the Wish Captors only caught properties relating to bears like the pointy muzzle, the round ears, the short tail, the soft fur, the large paws and so on. If the Wish Captor could catch more properties, not necessarily related to bears, it would open to more possibilities. This idea gave Faunour a whole new perspective and a happier outlook into the future. His existence no longer seemed so bleak but became interesting and he now did not have enough hours in the day. He used to think that days were far too long in this remote location in Alaska.

After Nelson became Anton's bear, Faunour and Harriet were less compatible. She transformed into a bear and back into a human every time she grew anxious, nervous or angry. This was, most of the time, because she resented being Faunour's slave. She was pleased to send the best teddy bears to Hugh because he was happier in his new role, giving joy to so many children in his small town. However, she was uncomfortable with Faunour's doting admiration.

Meanwhile, she returned secretly to the camp and watched the bears on the river, also keeping an eye out for any teddy bears who might fall into the snow, but since Robotbear had started to do the trips with his rocket ship these random episodes did not occur again.

Even though Faunour had been sent to Earth to see other animals, he had not seen many yet. Only the occasional grizzly bear roaming about in a distance. Therefore, when Nanuk pressed against the window with his muzzle trying to catch a smell of what was inside, Faunour shrieked:

"Hey! Who are you?"

Nanuk had rubbed his nose a little on the window to attract Faunour's attention. He nudged and put his nose to the window again.

Faunour got up. "A bear. Interesting. He must have smelled the presence of other bears," Faunour thought as he opened the door.

"Would you like to come in, bear?"

"Sure. Thank you, bear." And Nanuk wiped his paws on the mat before entering Faunour's small office. There was barely enough room for such a large polar bear. Faunour had not really been expecting full-sized bears in his little room. But the room adjusted to Nanuk's size and when the walls had stretched enough, Nanuk was inside and could warm up a little.

"Hello there, I am Nanuk," he said.

"Nice to meet you. Welcome. I am Faunour."

"And what do you do, Faunour?" Nanuk asked.

When Faunour explained to him that there was a planet for bears, Nanuk was rather intrigued and sat down. His white fur regained its fluffiness with the cozy heat in Faunour's office. Faunour offered him a cup of hot chocolate.

"A planet for bears? Really? What do the bears do there?"

"Mostly, they watch bears on Earth through telescopes. They also study the bear language and go for strolls in the Bear Parks."

"How do you get there?" Nanuk asked, because this description was very appealing.

Nanuk immediately wanted to go. Without hesitation, he thought that being on a bear planet could only be a serious improvement to his current situation on Earth.

"Go there? Well, I am not sure how real Earth bears can survive on Alas-K. And I haven't told you everything yet, Nanuk. However, if it is possible, you could take the rocket that brings the bears here. When the rocket goes back to the planet, it could take you to Alas-K."

"Oh, that would be wonderful!"

"Wonderful? Are you sure, Nanuk? There are a few requirements for the Alas-K bear that you should be aware of. You will lose your memory, your whole existence on Earth will be wiped out."

Nanuk put his paw under his chin and started thinking. "Mmm Hmmmm," he said to himself slowly, a few times in a row. "Losing my memory and my existence on Earth? A whole new world? A fresh start? Well, that doesn't sound bad at all." Nanuk took a sip from the hot chocolate and imagined the bear planet. It seemed like paradise to him.

"What do you mean the rocket brings the bears here? What bears?" Nanuk asked after taking a little moment to ponder over the bear planet.

"This is the other thing I am worried about. The Alas-K bears' main purpose is to become teddy bears for children on Earth. So, if you, a real Earth bear, move to Alas-K, perhaps you will also have to come back as a teddy bear yourself. Would you want that?"

"Mmmmh," said Nanuk and put his head in his paws. "I am not sure about that indeed. Becoming a teddy bear? Are you sure?"

"Well, the Alas-K bear yes, but I don't know about real live bears. I have to ask them up there on the planet about that."

"Yes, please. That would be very helpful to know."

Thinking about his lonely hunting days on Earth, Nanuk was very tempted to try out a new planet. Even if this would mean returning as a teddy bear.

"If it is at all possible, Faunour, I would be glad to go to Alas-K. Let me know if I can go there and stay."

"OK. If this is what you want, I will call Adelaide and ask her if we need to do something before you leave. This is very exciting indeed. I think you will be the first Earth bear ever that will travel to Alas-K!"

"Very exciting indeed, Faunour. Thank you so much. I will go now and think about it. I will come back to see you very soon."

"Great, Nanuk, good luck to you, and I will see you very soon. The next rocket will be here in a couple of weeks."

Nanuk raised his paw and lumbered away.

"Earth bears on Alas-K. Wow!"

Faunour was in awe.

Faunour calls Adelaide

On Alas-K, Adelaide had her paws full with the developing bears.

"Oh my, oh my, there is one with a not so pointy muzzle. How will you be able to do the Nuzzle properly?"

Adelaide circled a developing bear with great concern and looked at him very closely. His Wish Captor was blinking because the stars were catching more random wishes than usual.

All Wish Captors had a random percentage, as the math behind the wishes was not a totally exact science either. Sometimes wishes were blurred, the child did not know how to speak yet or did not shape the wish precisely so the stars on the Wish Captors for pointy muzzles sometimes caught wishes for rounded muzzles or bushy tails by mistake, or the wishes that landed on the Wish Captors were more or less undefined. Adelaide had to fix that and arrange the muzzles back to a pointy shape so the bear would be ready to do the Nuzzle with the Muzzle the best way possible.

Little Karu was one of the developing bears who had not received precise enough wishes for a pointy muzzle. He looked anxiously at Adelaide as she touched up his muzzle with a needle and a thread.

"Oh, don't worry. This won't hurt you." And she arranged the muzzle in such a way that it followed a straight line down from the bear's forehead.

"There you go, little Karu. You are all set."

Karu smiled and jumped happily from his seat.

The other Karus looked at her in great anticipation. They all had been created by wishes that came from a group of children of the planet Earth where the winters are long and cold and where it snows a lot.

From time to time, Adelaide had to touch up a muzzle here and an ear there. She was also in charge of the Nuzzle with the Muzzle training. The developing bears needed to learn how to do the famous Nuzzle in all possible ways and in all possible situations if they wanted to have the best chance to win the Nuzzle Competition.

The Nuzzle with the Muzzle was what a bear was made for. When the bears played with their child they put their nose on the child's cheek in such a fashion as to create pure happiness. And in order to do that properly the muzzle had to be a certain shape. As straight as possible, down from the forehead.

When they were all fixed, Adelaide called the Karus to remind them of the workshop they had to attend.

"This month's Nuzzle Competition is fast approaching. I need you to remember the basic steps of the Nuzzle motion."

The little bears sat down in a circle around Adelaide and looked at her attentively. At that moment, the screen in the middle of her workshop started ringing. That meant that there was some interplanetary communication happening.

Adelaide asked the bears to practice the Nuzzle quietly while she answered the call.

"Hello, Faunour!" Adelaide greeted him joyfully. She was always happy to hear from Faunour as she had been missing her friend a lot since he was sent to Earth.

"Hello, Adelaide. How is it going up there on the planet?"

"Oh, you know, just the usual. Some muzzles need touching up and we were about to start practicing a little for the Nuzzle with the Muzzle competition. What's up with you?"

"I have news for you!"

"Really? What is it?"

"I recently had the visit from a polar bear."

"A real polar bear?"

"Yes! He was wandering around in the snow and somehow he found my little office hidden in the snow."

"Was that the first real bear that you've encountered?"

"Yes, indeed. I have seen polar bears and grizzly bears from a distance, but never once has one come up to the cabin like that. This one came here, he even put his nose against the window!"

"Wow, that must have been frightening!" Adelaide said. "What did he want?"

"Oh, I think he was just curious at first, but then I told him about our planet, and he became very excited."

"Excited about what?"

"He wants to come to Alas-K and live there."

"Oh my, a real Earth bear?"

"Yes. I thought you'd find that noteworthy. And I wanted to ask you what he would need in order to travel safely?"

"Oh my, oh my, this would be the first time ever a real bear came to Alas-K, are you well aware of that, Faunour?" Adelaide was suddenly worried.

"Yes, yes, but do you think it will be safe for him to travel? His name is Nanuk."

"Oh, I will have to try and find out if we know anything about Earth bears coming to Alas-K, and how the Earth bear can become an Alas-K bear and I also might have to discuss this with President Teddy Bear first. But in principle, I believe that shouldn't be much of a problem. Alas-K is the bear planet after all, so why shouldn't it be open to Earth bears?"

"Thank you, Adelaide. Nanuk will be happy to hear that."

"Yes, but don't forget to tell him that he will forget everything once he comes to the planet, because Alas-K bears don't remember anything."

"Yes, Adelaide. I have already told him. He seems very upset about the lack of food here on Earth. These are tough times for polar bears because of the global warming."

"Global warming? Oh my, thank goodness we don't feel that here. Anyway, yes, tell him we will be honored and happy to welcome an Earth bear to Alas-K. Let me just talk to Teddy Bear first."

"OK, thank you, let me know what he says."

"Yes. Goodbye now."

"Until then!"

Adelaide rubbed her paw a little under her chin. A real Earth bear! Astonishing.

"Will he learn how to do the Nuzzle with us?" A little Karu asked.

Indeed, Adelaide wondered. She would have to teach a real Earth bear how to do the Nuzzle with the Muzzle.

Bear Observation Session on the planet Alas-K

Little Creamy had started the observation session of the bears early because it was a perfect day to watch bears on Earth. Some days were especially good for catching salmon which meant that the bears on the bear planet had to be more focused.

A few bears were still very sleepy because a loud alarm had dragged them out of bed. Although they don't feel much and remember even less, Alas-K bears very much enjoy a good night's sleep.

One little bear asked another "What is going on, why do we have to be at the Telescope Park so early?"

"I don't know. Maybe the bears on Earth are particularly active today? It is such a wonderful thing to see them on the river."

"Yes, it is. But I would really have liked to sleep in today. I am so tired."

"Yes, I know what you mean. When I catch a lot of wishes on a particular day, I feel so exhausted I can do hardly anything. They just keep coming and coming and then I have to lie down."

"Yes, I know that feeling."

"Bears! Please pay close attention to what I am going to say." Little Creamy had switched on the telescopes and dusted a little in front of them so the bears wouldn't step on too much planet stardust. Sometimes the dust on the planet could get in the way of their wish receiving capacity. Little Creamy was the newly appointed Observer in Chief of the Bear Observation session.

Little Creamy had a very special screwdriver. He wasn't aware of his magical quality, and he had even forgotten where he had found it. He used the screwdriver to fix the telescopes and most of the time he was annoyed because the screwdriver was so big and frequently fell out of his paws. But this screwdriver knew how to translate feelings and moods between beings of different kinds.

"Focus on the bears on the river please."

The bears all put their muzzles close to the eyepieces by looking down, so their eyes were at the level of the eyepiece. One of the reasons why their muzzles had to be straight from the forehead was that they had to be able to look into a telescope's eyepiece, any other kind of muzzle would make this very difficult and get in the way.

"Now look at the bears' shapes and take screen captures."

The bears adjusted the telescopes to the bears catching salmon on the river. Every few moments, they stopped to take a screenshot. That way, the bears' moves were registered step by step.

"This allows you to make flip-books. We need to follow their motion in order to keep in mind how a bear moves. When you become teddy bears, you will have to remember well how a bear moves."

The bears wondered why this was so important. Children could decide how they moved and the most important thing was the Nuzzle anyway. A few bears started yawning.

"Stay focused. We need to follow the bears and have a good image of the way they move. This is essential to the Nuzzle with the Muzzle. Only when we know really well how the real bears move can we do a proper Nuzzle."

"All right then," the bears stared very hard at the beautiful grizzly bears who were catching salmon in a river on the planet Earth.

"Aren't they magnificent?" Little Creamy made the round and checked on each telescope and was satisfied that they showed beautiful big grizzlies raising their paws and opening their mouths to catch fish.

"Yes, those are beautiful bears, Creamy."

"Once you are done, please come to the front and we will print out the screen captures."

Little Creamy got busy with the telescope printer and waited for it to produce a flip-book for each telescope. If one bear was not attentive enough and didn't push the screen capture button at a regular pace, the fluidity of the motion was off and the bear didn't appear to move slowly once the flip-books were put together. They would seem to be moving in saccades.

"Pay attention, Wilbur. You don't push at a regular pace. Watch the timer near the screen."

Wilbur had indeed dozed off periodically. He was very tired as he had caught particularly numerous wishes during the night. He was a white teddy and looked very much like a polar bear now.

"Sorry, Creamy. But I wonder why we usually only watch grizzlies. I really need to see a polar bear in order to shape up as one."

"Yes, I understand, I can see that you got a lot of polar bear wishes. I will try to get us a polar bear angle for the next time."

"Oh, that would be wonderful!" Wilbur said, paying closer attention now to take the screen captures in the right rhythm.

"Oh, Creamy, could we one day zoom in on a zoo? We could maybe catch a glimpse of many different bears. And other animals, too?"

"What are you talking about? How do you even know about zoos?" Little Creamy got very frightened. He knew what happened when the bears started talking about other animals. President Teddy Bear did not like that at all.

The little bear who had spoken was hiding his muzzle behind the eyepiece of the telescope. "Sorry, Creamy. I might have heard about it from Bearmouse."

"Oh, I see. Bearmouse knows a lot about other animals." Little Creamy was relieved. If other bears had found the path to the Secret Library, he didn't know what would happen.

Wishing for Love

Harriet had just come home from her bear watching session of the day. She was exhausted. There had been many more bears at the river than usual and she had taken many notes. All her observations were now being used by the bear watchers on the planet Alas-K, and Little Creamy was grateful for Harriet's accurate bear descriptions. They helped with the flip-book making and allowed for more organized bear observation sessions.

"Hey, Faunour, how was your day?" Harriet asked cheerfully on her way in. She wiped her snow boots on the mat and expected a gloomy reply as usual. But Faunour ran to the door to greet her. He hugged her and jumped for joy.

"Oh my, this is unusual. Look at you! Why are you so cheerful?" Harriet laughed and hugged him back. "What happened?"

"Harriet! Exciting news! A real polar bear came to the house!"

"What? A polar bear? Are you serious? There are no polar bears around here! I have to go on another expedition to see them!" She became irritable and quickly slipped into her bear state.

"Wait, wait, Harriet. No need to get angry! Nanuk is a live polar bear who has traveled here from the pack ice over at the island. He was looking for food, and somehow he found our little house. I suppose he slipped into Imagination to find us, as we are now invisible to the surroundings."

Harriet calmed down a little and took a sip from the hot white chocolate Faunour had put in her hands. Her hands had turned to paws and she was sitting on the couch in her bear state, taking a deep breath. The hot chocolate didn't quite taste the same when she was a bear. A tiny moment of irritation was enough to turn her into a bear.

"So, tell me, what did Nanuk want?"

"You will not believe this. Nanuk wants to move to Alas-K!"

"But he already lives here."

"No, our Alas-K, the planet Alas-K, the planet of bears!"

"Oh, I see. That Alaska."

"Alas-K. With a K."

"Yeah, yeah, Alas-K. Why does he want to do that? Did you tell him that he would lose his memory and become a teddy bear?"

"I did, actually. And it didn't seem to bother him."

"OK then, did you ask Teddy Bear and Adelaide what to do?"

"Yes, I have. Adelaide has to ask Teddy Bear and the others. I just wanted you to know as soon as you came home."

"Thanks, Faunour."

Harriet started thinking that if an Earth bear could go to the planet Alas-K, so could she.

She began to feel butterflies in her stomach.

The Kitchen Giraffe is created

"This is very strange, you see," the Kitchen Giraffe said out loud. These words sounded very strange to her ears because they were the first words she had ever pronounced out loud. Those were also the very first words she had started to put together in her head before she pronounced them.

She looked around. There were trees and flowers and green grass. It looked like a forest. Green meadows with flowers of all kinds separated rows of thicker trees from light. "This must be a glade," she thought. She was sitting at the border of light and darkness, to one side there was light and to the other a darker area with more trees that gave more shadow. She quickly moved her head from one side to the other and tried to mix the light with the dark. Once she got tired of this game, she got up and walked a little along the border of sun and shadow. She thought the space in-between was particularly lovely. She could stick out her head to the side of the light and then refresh her head in the dark shadow of the trees, so she walked a little moving her head from one side to the other and feeling more comfortable as she walked along.

Meanwhile, the Famous Wood Hound took that morning's blueberry pie out of the oven. "Mmm, how delicious!" he thought, and put it on one of the pie stands where there was still room. The stands were already full of many other pies and the strawberry pies were especially delicious today. He had picked the fruit in the garden earlier.

The Wood Hound wiped his paws on his apron and sat down behind the counter.

He looked outside and wondered how things could be elsewhere in the world. He started dreaming about other places and wished he could travel as well. All the animals that came to see him wished to travel somewhere and with the help of his pies, they could see parallel worlds, places he was never allowed to see. He provided the means to go there, but he himself had to stay in the Woods of the Same Name.

"Why is that?" He asked aloud.

He began walking around his pie stands and looked closely at them. Sometimes, sparks and sizzling stars were flickering around them. "Which one of you could make me travel a little? I would like to visit another planet. I would not want to stay there forever, because I will take care of my pies, but I would sure like to see a bit of the world."

The Kitchen Giraffe had walked enough for her taste and was sighing deeply. "What now?" She asked. And then she came to a crossroads.

"Of course, those always come along when you need them."

She batted her eyelashes at the signpost and looked closely at the letters written on the two arrows. One sign read "Ademar's Famous Woodf Pie Bakery, 1 $^3/_4$ miles. Welcome to another world." and the other read "Faunour, 1 $^3/_4$ miles. Join the MOLOB! Liberate the Bears." That one was pointing to the opposite direction.

"Well, they are both equally distant, so I will need to follow my intuition. My intuition? Well, I don't know what that is, you see."

She looked around, mumbling and talking to herself. After a little while, she decided to close her eyes, to concentrate and breathe, and think very hard about which was the best way to go. She sat down.

"Whee Hee Heee!" Someone said and interrupted her concentration. It was impossible to tell how much time had elapsed. But she was still sitting there, in front of the signpost, thinking hard about which way to go.

The Kitchen Giraffe slowly opened her big eyes.

"Whee Hee Hee!" She heard the same sound again and slowly turned around.

"Well, hello there!" the animal said.

"Hello. Who are you?"

"That is an excellent question. I am not quite sure. But I am a horse, I think."

"You think?"

"Yes, I think. Horses make this sound. "Whee Hee Hee!"

"If you say so."

"And you, who are you?"

"That is a very good question, Horse. I think I am a giraffe. But you see, the stripes on my coat make me a zebra. So, I am a bit confused myself."

The horse looked at the giraffe's stripes very closely. "Beautiful pattern."

"Thank you, Horse." The giraffe batted her eyelashes at him.

Blushing a little, the horse asked: "What are you doing here?"

"I am at a crossroads. So, I am thinking about which way to go."

"I see. Do you *have* to go somewhere?"

"Of course I do. When you are at a crossroads, you have to choose which way to go, don't you?"

"I don't know. Why can't we stay here?"

The giraffe put her front hoof to her head to help her think.

"I don't know. Maybe we can stay here for a while. Why don't you sit down and think about it with me?"

"OK, I will do that." And the horse sat down next to the giraffe.

"Close your eyes and breathe. And concentrate. It is a lot of fun," she said.

"Now, what do I concentrate on?"

"Whatever you'd like. But if you need inspiration, look at the signpost first."

The horse looked closely at the two signs right in front of them.

"Woof Pie Bakery. That sounds wonderful. I certainly would like to eat pie. I am very hungry."

"Yes, I was in favor of the Famous Bakery myself. I am not so sure I would like to save bears. I don't know much about bears. And I am not sure if I like them, you see. Do *you* like them?"

The horse shook his mane, breathed out the way horses do, and thought about it for a little while.

"Bears. Let me think. Yes, I like them, yes. I am pretty sure that I do. I believe there is one special bear that I actually need to see. But things are not very clear in my head. Maybe you are right, and I need to focus a little first."

The horse and the giraffe both closed their eyes and started breathing and thinking and concentrating together.

After a while of doing that, the horse opened one eye and looked at the giraffe. She was still sitting there with her eyes closed, breathing and concentrating.

"You have a lovely hat."

"Oh my, thank you, Horse. It is my blue funnel hat. I have always had it and I don't know what it is good for."

"Maybe it is just good for being pretty."

She smiled. "Yes, maybe." And she closed her eyes again.

"You know what," the Horse said, "this is a lovely place, maybe we can stay here forever?"

"Yes, it is lovely, isn't it? It is the most beautiful clearing I have ever seen. Well actually, it is also the first one I have been to."

"Yes, I agree. And I don't recall having seen much before this either."

And they both closed their eyes again and focused and breathed some more.

After a while, the giraffe opened one eye and looked at the horse. "You have a beautiful mane. Beautiful ivory color. And the white stripe on your nose is quite attractive as well."

"Thank you, Giraffe." The horse smiled and opened both his eyes.

"You know what, I think we should go to the bakery. I am a little hungry now and I have a feeling that Ademar might be able to help us. Perhaps he even knows who we are," the giraffe said.

"OK, let's do that," the horse said and they both got up and chose the path that led to the Woof Pie Bakery.

Ademar, King of the Forest of the Same Name

After walking exactly 1 ¾ miles, the giraffe and the horse arrived at a little house. It was painted bright red and on its bright blue door was a sign that read "Come in!"

"Let's go in, then." The giraffe looked at the horse and he nodded. So, they both went inside.

Immediately, Ademar jumped up from his seat to welcome them.

"Hello, you two. I am so glad that you are here! I am Ademar, and this is the Wood Pie Factory."

"Hello, Ademar. I am so pleased to meet you, too! I thought this place was called the Woof Pie Bakery," the giraffe said.

"Yes, you are right, I am sorry. I have a little difficulty choosing the right name. Or remembering it. This is the Forest of the Same Name, so it is difficult to put the right name on things, because they tend to all have the same name, you understand."

"Well, well, well. No, I don't think I understand, you see," the giraffe said.

"That's OK, neither do I," the dachshund said and shook her hoof gracefully.

"Whee Hee Hee," the horse said.

"Hello, Appropriate Horse. I know someone who will be very happy to see you," Ademar said and shook the Horse's hoof enthusiastically.

"Hello, Ademar. Why do you call me appropriate horse?"

"That's because you are. You are the Appropriate Horse that the Knight of the Round Ear has been wishing for."

"Ah." The Appropriate Horse started scratching his mane. "Ah" was all he could think of saying.

"How do you know that?"

"Oh, you know, Appropriate Horse, there are things that I know that just happen to come together here and make sense once the thing they name arrives. I know that you are the Appropriate Horse because you are."

"I believe you. We have actually come here because we hoped you would know who we are."

"You have come to the right place, then. You are the Kitchen Giraffe. Named after a kitchen tool, a stick blender. Do you know what you came here for?"

"Not really," the Kitchen Giraffe said. "The other sign where we started said something about bears. Liberate the bears or something like that. Do you know something about it?"

"Sure. The MOLOB. The liberation movement of bears created by Faunour. He is a bear from the planet Alas-K and he sends teddy bears to children all over the world."

"Bears come from the teddy bear planet?"

"Yes, they are created by wishes on the planet and then they travel to Earth."

"And what does Faunour do?"

"He welcomes them to Alaska, removes the Wish Captors and sends them off to their new homes with the children who wished for them."

"That seems like an interesting system," the Horse said. "Do the bears on the planet also wish for things?"

"Yes, they do. And that's why you are here," Ademar said.

"From Alas-K to Alaska. Sounds like fun! The same name, again," the giraffe said.

"It sounds like a nice planet, a planet of wishes. Maybe we should visit?" the Horse suggested.

"Absolutely," Ademar said enthusiastically. "I have just been thinking about a place to visit. And you, Appropriate Horse, you could take us there in no time as you are being wished for."

"Whee Hee Hee. Will we become bears? Will we get a Wish Captor?"

"I am not sure. I, for one, will only visit as I have this Bakery to take care of. And the pies that I bake are used for travel between worlds. But you two, I believe you can choose whether you want to stay or not, as you don't have a home yet. I believe that I can take us to Alas-K without Faunour and without the rocket. We just have to choose the right pie and wish for it in a pure and focused way."

"Bears. Well, I am not so sure I like them very much. They are solitary and rude and have no manners." The Kitchen Giraffe adjusted her funnel hat and batted her lashes.

The dog and the horse laughed. "You will be safe. We will protect you."

And the three of them focused very hard on the planet Alas-K, wishing to be there.

"Wait!" Ademar said. "We need to eat some pie first."

"Wee Hee Hee. I thought you'd never suggest it. I am starving!" And they listened to the Horse's growling stomach.

"Mmmm. All those beautiful pies," the giraffe said, smelling the beautiful, colorful pies on the stands. "Which one should I choose?"

The Horse chose the apple pie because horses love apples.

After examining the fruit pie stands carefully, the giraffe turned her head to the quiche stands where the pies contained vegetables rather than fruit.

"Oh, the broccoli quiche looks fabulous!" And the broccoli quiche started glowing right away. The giraffe took a piece and started chewing on it with delight.

The Famous Wood Hound did not hesitate, he knew exactly that his personal favorite was the blueberry pie, and a piece jumped right into his mouth.

"Mmmm. Are we all set now?"

The giraffe and the horse nodded. And all three of them held hooves and paws, closed their eyes and wished to be on the planet Alas-K.

And there they were, four bright stars that lit up in front of them and led them out of the bakery through the Imagination onward to a new world.

"Oh, this is so exciting, you see," said the Kitchen Giraffe before all three of them were being swallowed by the Imagination.

Private Meeting about welcoming new bears from Earth

Adelaide had called President Teddy Bear and Bearmouse, Little Creamy, Big Creamy, the Secretary of Puzzlement from the Department of Astonishing Things, Hector, the Bear Image Secretary, and Faufur, Professor of the Bear Language, co-inventor of the Nuzzle with the Muzzle and knowledgeable about Magic Potions, for a private meeting. All these bears occupied key positions on the planet as they used to be teddy bears on Earth. Therefore, none of them had a Wish Captor.

President Teddy Bear was the oldest teddy bear on Alas-K. He knew most of the secrets of the planet and was very concerned with keeping the bear planet a planet for bears only. There were speculations that this attitude came from a long time ago when his child had abandoned him for a bunny. Indeed, Teddy Bear hated the planet Alas-L, where the bunnies lived, more than anything and was afraid that bunnies would one day come and invade the bear planet.

He had, therefore, developed a restrictive attitude to who was or was not allowed to come and live on the planet.

Faufur on the other hand was a young bear who had once been a child's favorite toy. Faufur was Faunour's brother which meant that they were of the same teddy bear kind. They were both created out of nothing. Whereas Faufur had been chosen by a child, Faunour had not yet been to Earth as a teddy bear. Faufur taught the Bear Language on the planet which was sometimes far too complicated even for him so he had to rest a lot.

Adelaide had invited them to the conference room to present the case of Nanuk and the news of Earth bears on Alas-K.

Bearmouse was very eager to know all about it.

"So, tell me what did he say? What does he look like? Will he fit in the rocket?"

"Slow down, Bearmouse. First let me welcome you. Thank you all for joining me here at this meeting. President. Professor Faufur. Little Creamy. Hector. Big Creamy."

They all nodded and Bearmouse took a deep breath to give himself patience.

"Faunour has called to tell me about a real polar bear named Nanuk who would like to come to Alas-K and live here with us. Do you think this is possible?"

"I think he might need some Magic Potion," Faufur said immediately.

"Wait, Faufur. We must tread carefully with the Magic Potions. They are hidden all over the planet. Some of them can only be used for extreme emergencies. They maintain the parallel worlds in balance. So, in order to get to them and to use some of them, we need to really think about it very hard," President Teddy Bear said.

And all seven bears put their heads in their paws and concentrated very hard on the subject.

After a while, Adelaide said "I know! We can just wait and see what happens."

Bearmouse said "I will invite Nanuk to my talk show and he will tell us about his experience."

Faufur said "He will enroll in the next Bear Language session and perhaps we will learn how Earth bears talk."

Faufur was always interested in learning new Bear Dialects. The language of bears had many varieties. Now with Nanuk, he was hoping to learn a real Alaskan dialect.

Little Creamy said "He will learn how to watch bears on Earth and I am sure he can give us precious indications about them. But before he leaves Earth, it would be wonderful to be able to watch him in his natural surroundings first." Little Creamy thought about Wilbur's suggestion.

"Yes, because he will probably lose his memory once he joins us here." Bearmouse objected.

"That is true," Teddy Bear said. "We can ask the Knight of the Round Ear what he thinks would be the appropriate Magic Potion in this case."

Adelaide thought she should have asked him to their meeting, too.

"Yes, I will go and see him and ask."

Wapusk

"Everybody welcome to the Nuzzle Competition Training! I hope Adelaide has fixed all your muzzles and we can begin. You learn the technique with Adelaide but the volume training is with me. You need to practice a lot of repetitions to become real masters of the Nuzzle with the Muzzle which is what bears are famous for and why they are wished for by so many children. This Nuzzle Training on our planet is unique and our only way to compete against the bunnies that now take our place in many homes."

At this point in his speech, the Knight of the Round Ear paused and looked at the bears who were sitting side by side forming rows. They now had a distinct surprised look on their faces. If sadness had been known on the planet, the bears would have looked sad.

"Wapusk!" One bear suddenly cried out.

"What did you say?"

"Wapusk!"

"What does that mean?"

"I don't know. It just came to my mind. Wapusk."

The Knight of the Round Ear adjusted his visor and thought aloud. "Wapusk. I think I have heard that word before." He went to the cabinet with his Magic Potions. He checked the rows with the bottles of various colors very slowly and very carefully, paying attention to his visor so it wouldn't close because he wanted to see the labels.

"Wapusk means white bear." Adelaide had arrived at the Nuzzle Training Hall and had overheard the last few words spoken. "In one of the languages on Earth spoken by Natives I believe."

"Adelaide! Welcome to the Nuzzle Training," said the Knight. "The bears are ready to start. I see you did some great work in touching up their muzzles and ears. What brings you here?"

"Oh, Knight. I have great news. A real Earth bear would like to come to our planet. A white bear. A Wapusk actually. A polar bear, as they are called on Earth."

"Are you serious? A real live Earth bear will be joining us here? Did you hear that, bears?"

Some bears said "Ah!" and some said "Oh!" some of them cheered and some of them seemed worried, and others didn't seem to care much about real live bears, they were impatient to start the training and tried out the Nuzzle on the bear sitting next to them. The bears who received the Nuzzle giggled with pleasure.

"Yes, and so I wanted to ask you if you have a Magic Potion especially for him. We could give it to Robotbear when he returns to Earth. He will bring Nanuk back here next time he delivers the bears to Faunour."

"Oh, I understand. I think I know now why the word Wapusk came up. Wapusky is the name of the potion he will need. I will get it for you."

The word Wapusk had triggered the thread to the right Magic Potion and the Knight went back to the cabinet to get it. The bottle was pink and the label was blue. It said Wapusky.

"Here you go, Adelaide. I am very happy to hear that we will have a new kind of bear on our planet soon. Teddy Bear won't mind I suppose as it is a bear. I know how reluctant he is to accept other animals. If only we had my Appropriate Horse. Everything would be much easier."

The bears giggled again. When the Knight mentioned his Appropriate Horse, nobody knew what that meant. The Knight didn't like it when others laughed at him for his wish, so he started to blow his whistle.

"Quiet, bears. Start with the first position now. Focus. Nose on the cheek. Practice with your neighbor."

Adelaide took the potion carefully in her paw. "Thank you, Knight. This is lovely. I am sure your Appropriate Horse will come to the planet soon."

The Knight was absorbed in his training, but he smiled inside his helmet and he blinked gratefully at Adelaide for understanding. His visor closed and made the "Clong!" sound.

Little Creamy calls Faunour

Nanuk had stayed close to the invisible little cabin where Faunour was working on the Wish Captors. He had thought long and hard about moving to the bear planet and had decided that it would be a wonderful adventure. He was on his way back to Faunour's.

Faunour was sitting at his desk, working on the Wish Captors. 'They should be able to catch many properties, not only bear properties,' he thought once again.

Meanwhile on the planet Alas-K, Little Creamy was on his way to the television room to call Faunour. He connected the screen and waited.

Faunour was startled by the sound of the communication. He answered the call, a little confused.

"Hello?"

"Hello, Faunour. Little Creamy speaking."

Faunour rubbed his eyes and recognized Little Creamy holding his huge screwdriver in one paw.

"Little Creamy! What a lovely surprise! I was working on the Wish Captors. You scared me just now, the place is all quiet. Harriet is asleep. The bears are in their boxes."

"I am sorry I startled you, but I have something important to ask you."

"Yes? Go ahead, ask."

"Adelaide has told us about Nanuk, a polar bear who wants to come to the bear planet."

"Yes, indeed, I am actually expecting him back any minute. I told him he should come back and I will let him know. Do you know if it is ok? I haven't heard from Adelaide yet."

"I think she had to ask the Knight of the Round Ear for a potion first. But I wanted to know something for my bear observation."

"Yes?"

"As you know, we only watch grizzlies most of the time. But we also have white bears developing on the planet. They receive wishes and turn into polar bears. But as we don't often see polar bears their shape cannot adjust properly, so do you think we could ask Nanuk to move around a little for us so the white bears can watch him before he comes here?"

"Oh, yes of course. I am sure he would love that very much. I will see if I can find him."

And Faunour put on a little coat and went outside. "Nanuk!" He called out. "Are you there?"

Nanuk was playing in the snow keeping an eye on the place where the house was. He couldn't see the house all the time as it was under the Automatic Negation spell, so from time to time there was a flicker and the house appeared, which was a relief to him every time he saw it. He thought that his lonely days would soon be over. Soon he would move to a place where many bears lived and he was looking forward to the adventures that awaited him. When Faunour called out to him he jumped up with joy. "Faunour! Over here!"

Now the house was in plain sight and he could safely approach it. Meanwhile, Little Creamy stared at the empty screen in anxious anticipation.

"Come over here, please. Little Creamy has a favor to ask you."

"Little Creamy?"

Nanuk was intrigued and quickly moved closer to the entrance where he could see Faunour standing wearing his red coat.

"Please come inside, Nanuk, I want you to meet someone. Little Creamy is the Engineer at the Maintenance of Telescopes, or Observer-in-chief of bears on the planet Alas-K!"

Nanuk entered the house that was now the right size for him. He wiped his paws and stretched a little.

"Come on in, Nanuk, don't be shy."

And facing the screen, Faunour added: "Little Creamy, this is Nanuk."

Faunour tilted the screen so that Little Creamy could see Nanuk.

"Oh my goodness, what a beautiful bear! Hello, Nanuk, I am so very pleased to meet you!"

Little Creamy was very excited to see a real polar bear.

"Hello, Little Creamy. I am very pleased to meet you, too. What did you want to ask me?"

"As Faunour might have told you, we bears on the planet Alas-K watch bears on Earth. Mostly grizzlies, but we rarely have the chance to see a polar bear."

"Oh, I suppose it is because there are not many of us left," Nanuk said with a sad tone.

"Why is that?" Little Creamy said, alarmed.

"You must have heard about global warming. Our ice is melting and we don't find enough seals. But enough about me, why do you need my help?"

"Nanuk, I need you to be available for a bear watch session so that my bears can see you move."

"What do you mean? What should I do?"

"Nothing in particular, just walk and play, things you would normally do."

"I understand, when and where would that be?"

"How about tomorrow morning? Will you be at the house? We would start our observation session with you!"

"Sure thing, Little Creamy," Nanuk said. "I would be honored."

Faunour smiled and patted Nanuk on the back.

"Thank you, Nanuk. And thanks, Little Creamy. I will sign off now and tell Nanuk a little more about his travels to Alas-K."

"All right, we will talk tomorrow then."

" Goodbye now." And Faunour switched the screen off.

"Oh, Nanuk, this is your first job for the planet Alas-K, I hope you realize that. It is wonderful that they thought about observing you first, don't you think?"

"Sure. Tell me about this observation of bears."

"It has to do with the shape the bears become. They can only become bears when they know what bears on Earth look like and how they move, so they have to study them. I must also tell you about the Wish Captors."

"What are those?"

"The Wish Captors are boxes with stars on them that are attached to the bear's tummy. When the Wish Captor has caught enough wishes, a bear wearing it can become a teddy bear. Then there is Nuzzle Training and a Competition after which the bears can be sent to Earth. When they arrive here, I remove their Wish Captors. I even have one myself."

"Can I see?" Nanuk asked.

Faunour stretched a little to show Nanuk his Wish Captor.

"I don't see any wishes," Nanuk put his muzzle close to Faunour's tummy. "Is it empty?"

"Yes, it is. There are no wishes for me yet. But some day, perhaps. Nelson told me that one day I may also become someone's teddy bear."

"And this is something to look forward to?"

"Of course. Then my life will be complete, I will experience full happiness because I will be in a place where I am totally wanted, the perfect place."

"I see. But won't you be dependent on someone? And will you wish for that in quite the same way?"

Nanuk was making a serious objection to the Wish Captor that Faunour had not thought about before. Nanuk would shake things up quite a bit on the bear planet.

"You are right, Nanuk. The Wish Captor works only in one direction. But we think that if someone wishes for you with all their heart, you will be happy in their company, even if you did not know it beforehand."

"Maybe you are right." Nanuk put his big paw to his chin and reflected a little on the subject. "So what are the Wish Captors for?"

"They make the bear complete so to speak. They catch the wishes from children and all people who wish for bears."

"Only bears?"

"Well, this is something we can discuss some other time. On the planet of bears, yes, the wishes are only about bears. But they need to have a connection to reality as well, so there is a Telescope Park where all the developing bears watch the bears on Earth."

"And why do you remove them?"

"I remove the Wish Captors from the teddy bears when they come here because they don't need them anymore, they are ready for their new homes."

Nanuk realized that there were more and more exciting facts about this new planet he still had to discover.

"So, can I go?"

"I think you can. Robotbear will be here soon with the next bear delivery and I am sure you can go back with him."

"Fantastic!" Nanuk jumped up and touched the ceiling a little with the top of his head. "Ouch!"

"Careful, careful. So, I will see you tomorrow morning then?"

"Yes. Good night, Faunour. And thank you for everything."

Nanuk slowly went outside and climbed into his den right outside the invisible house. He soon fell asleep, dreaming happily about the new and exciting life he would have as an AlasKan bear.

Christmas Nuzzle Competition

Everyone was getting ready for the Nuzzle Fest. It was always a great moment on the planet and the bears who had not competed this time left their observation posts and quickly made their way to the Main Hall.

The Nuzzle Fest was a big celebration and all the bears who had full Wish Captors were competing in it. This month, the Karus were all very excited because they had received the largest number of wishes and had scored the most pleasure points at the Nuzzle Training with the Knight of the Round Ear. Everybody was cheering them on.

All the important bears were there. President Teddy Bear had a little trouble with his monocle and his eye because of all the excitement, so Professor Faufur offered him a little bit of Imaginary Honey Salmon, the special treat at those events.

Big Creamy kept his pen and book ready in case anything puzzling might occur.

Little Creamy tried to keep his balance with his huge screwdriver and maintained a watchful eye on the bears who watched the other bears.

Hector, the Bear Image Secretary, closely watched the general appearance of all the bears. The nuzzles and the ears mostly, and he checked if they were all in a good shape. He also lent Bearmouse a paw with his show. Bearmouse reported on the Nuzzle Festival every time, and everyone in the Imagination was impatient to see the Nuzzle Festival of the month.

Adelaide and the Knight of the Round Ear had all the shirts ready for the competing bears.

Everyone was waiting for the signal to start.

The Knight of the Round Ear looked around, his visor permitting, and blew a long blast on his whistle.

Then, everyone held their breaths, while they waited for the competition to begin.

Bears had formed pairs and looked closely at each other before they started to do the nuzzle to each other. All the Wish Captors were almost completely full with wishes, so they were blinking in many different colors. When the nuzzle reached a peak in pleasure points, the Wish Captor started ringing and this was the sign that designated the winner of this month's Nuzzling Competition.

After a lot of giggling and muzzle rubbing, one bear finally had his Wish Captor ringing. It was the first Karu that Adelaide had fixed the other day.

Everyone jumped up from their seats and clapped their hands.

"We have a winner!" The Knight of the Round Ear announced. And he raised the paw of the little Karu whose Wish Captor had rung first.

Then they walked around in a circle so that everyone could admire Karu's pointy muzzle, rounded ears and cuddly body. He giggled and jumped around happily.

"I am proud to announce Karu as the winner of the Christmas Competition. He will be the first bear that will be delivered in a proper manner to Faunour for the Christmas Celebration on Earth. All the other Karus will join him."

Everyone applauded and cheered. Robotbear greeted the winner with a solemn handshake. "Karu I am honored…" And Karu laughed and giggled and jumped and was just about the happiest bear in the universe.

Watching Nanuk move

The next morning, Nanuk woke up early and, full of happy anticipation, ran over to the invisible house. He knocked on the door.

Harriet was slowly waking up. She checked if she was a bear or a woman and noticed that she was a woman. She smiled and put on a purple robe. The color matched her eyes and she thought how wonderful it would be to fall in love again. Suddenly, she heard knocking. She went to the door and opened it slowly, peeking outside. The snow whirled about and got caught in her hair.

"Hey, who are you?" Harriet asked.

"I am Nanuk, a polar bear."

"Hello Nanuk. Yes, I have heard about you. Are we expecting you?"

"Yes, you are. Well, Faunour is. And Little Creamy. They asked me to move around so they can watch me."

Nanuk moved about like a bear and put his nuzzle in the snow, then raised it in the air and struck a pose. Harriet laughed.

"Very well. Come on in, Nanuk. I am Harriet. I am... well...I am... here to help Faunour."

"Pleased to meet you. You are not a bear, though."

"Well, not today, no. But some days, I am."

"I see," said Nanuk who didn't really see what she meant.

"Anyway, come on in. Faunour must be expecting you."

Nanuk lumbered in and paid careful attention to act in a bearish manner. Harriet watched him and laughed. "Be natural, Nanuk. You don't have to *act* a bear - you *are* a bear!"

Nanuk turned around to look at Harriet. "Yes, you are right. I am a real bear!"

"Yes, you are. I will see if Faunour has set up the communication with the planet already."

Harriet knocked on Faunour's door.

"Yes, come in." Faunour called.

"Come on, Nanuk. I think they are ready for you."

Nanuk looked at Harriet and she pushed him gently into the room. "You'll be great."

"Hello there, Nanuk. Welcome. Look, Little Creamy and the bears at the Telescope Park are all waiting for you."

Nanuk put his muzzle closer to the screen. The bears on the planet Alas-K were in awe.

"Look, a real polar bear in Faunour's office! Amazing. Astonishing."

"Puzzling, I would say," said the Secretary of Puzzlement who had joined the Bear Observation session for the occasion. He had sensed that something puzzling was about to happen. He immediately started to write it down in his Book of Puzzlement.

Nanuk moved around, sat down and turned around. The bears laughed and clapped their hands.

"Faunour, can you step outside? We want to see Nanuk in the snow."

"Of course!" Faunour said, and he took the screen outside with him.

"Come on, Nanuk. Run around outside a little to show them what a polar bear looks like playing in the snow."

Nanuk tried to act as natural as possible but couldn't resist taking a few poses and raising his muzzle in the air as if to smell something.

The bears were impressed. They had never enjoyed such a special treat before.

"Thank you, Faunour. I have recorded this, so our bears, like Wilbur here, can study how the polar bears move."

Wilbur was very pleased, having noticed a stronger outline to his shape already.

"Thank you, Nanuk. Thank you, Faunour. We will leave you now. Robotbear needs help preparing the bears for their journey to Earth. Nanuk, we will see you soon on our planet!"

Nanuk waved his paw and looked happily at the screen. He was not completely aware that his existence on Earth would soon be ended and that a whole new life awaited him.

Christmas Delivery

Robotbear had again borrowed Little Creamy's screwdriver to tighten the screws on the rocket. The rocket giggled as usual.

"Hey, Robotbear, we are all going to Earth for Christmas! Yeah!" The large group of Karus jumped up and down on their way to the rocket.

"Congratulations. Being a Christmas bear is indeed one of the highest honors." Robotbear congratulated the Karus on their success. The Karus had to be the most joyful and happy bears he had ever shipped to Earth.

"You know that you will fall asleep on your way to Earth, so please get into the boxes right away."

The Karus excitedly jumped into the boxes.

"Everything ready? Is everybody here?"

"Yeh!" They cried.

"Wait, wait, wait. Please don't forget this. And take good care of it." Adelaide came running to the cockpit with the

Magic Potion especially chosen for Nanuk. "You will need this to give to Nanuk before you bring him to the planet. Please, don't forget."

"Of course not, Adelaide. You know that my memory is just fine," Robotbear said with his robot voice.

Adelaide laughed. "Fine, then have a safe flight, all of you. And bring back the lovely Nanuk safely."

"Thank you. Goodbye!"

Robotbear waved goodbye to Adelaide and the whole group that was standing on the platform. Even Teddy Bear had come to say goodbye. The notion of going to Earth for Christmas had moved Teddy Bear and even stirred up some fond memories. But as he couldn't concentrate on the exact nature of these memories, he remained in a vague state of mind and bid farewell to the rocket. The rocket let a light slide on her side and they were on their way.

Getting Nanuk ready for the planet of the bears

In Faunour's office, everyone was celebrating, Faunour and Harriet had invited Nanuk and his brothers to ready themselves for the big departure. Nanuk wanted to say goodbye to his family, and his two brothers had come over from the island for the occasion. They were very excited to help Nanuk set up for the trip.

Nanuk was running around in circles. He didn't fully grasp the end of his existence on Earth and he was starting to feel quite anxious.

"Please, Nanuk, calm down, the rocket will be here any minute and we need to collect the bears. You will have plenty of time to adjust. Just remember that you will forget your past life here on Earth once you arrive on Alas-K."

"But, Harriet, that makes no sense! How can I remember that I will forget? It is a contradiction," Nanuk said, feeling more and more worried about his decision being the right one.

"Nothing grows in the comfort zone," one of his brothers said.

"Since when did you start using inspirational quotes?" Nanuk snapped.

"I don't know, brother. It seemed appropriate."

"I am not so sure about the comfort zone anymore."

"It is the values that count," said his other brother.

"You, too?" Nanuk became a little irritated.

"Calm down, Nanuk. You are a celebrity. They will treat you like a king on the planet. No other bear has ever done what you are about to do," Faunour said. "I am very proud to know you."

"But I am not a hero," protested Nanuk, becoming even more nervous.

"You will meet many different bears. And you will not feel hungry. On the planet, there are no emotions, no bad sensations."

"No sensations? Oh my, Harriet what am I doing? Do you think this is a good idea?"

"Yes, Nanuk, you are very brave. And you being there will make the whole universe better. Even the parallel worlds will be in better harmony."

"Why do you say that?"

"Because any act of courage adds to the harmony of the whole."

"Now you are wise-cracking, too."

"Sorry, Nanuk. We are just trying to cheer you up."

While they were reassuring Nanuk, the rocket began its slow approach to Alaska. Robotbear checked on the Karus who were now a lot less noisy and joyful than before.

"Are we almost there?" They asked, yawning and stretching and curling up in their boxes.

"Yes, you can go back to sleep now. It is all good. I can see the landing platform from here. Faunour and Harriet must be waiting for us."

The Karus were happy, and went back to sleep.

Robotbear put the rocket carefully down on the landing spot and turned the engine off.

Harriet ran outside to greet them.

When Robotbear got out of the rocket, he was surprised to see Harriet in her bear state.

"Well, hello there, what a perky looking bear you are!"

"Why thank you, Robotbear. How was the flight?"

"It was good. I have brought you the Christmas bears. They are called Karu. You will recognize the winner of the Nuzzle Competition. He is bigger and softer and cuddlier than the others, but they are all wonderful."

"I am sure they are. Please go inside, Robotbear. Nanuk is anxious to meet you. I will take care of the Karus."

The rocket beeped a little to greet Harriet and opened the cargo hold for her. Harriet switched back into her woman shape and took out the boxes of Karus.

Robotbear went into the house.

Faunour was excited to see him and hugged him. Robotbear hugged him back. "Hello, Faunour. This is a big day for all of us. Where is Nanuk? I need to give him something."

Nanuk was hiding in the office. He was having a severe panic attack.

Robotbear knocked and went in.

"Hey, Nanuk. What is the matter with you? Aren't you excited? We are all looking forward to having you on the planet of bears. Bearmouse has invited you to his next show and he is very pleased to welcome a real polar bear. Don't be afraid. Our planet is wonderful."

"Is it? And how will I survive? Is that even possible?"

"Good that you ask. I have something for you."

"What is it?"

"It is a Magic Potion, especially designed for you. It is called Wapusky."

"Wapusk, that's us. That means polar bear!"

"You see. Everything will be all right. You take a few drops of the potion and you will be perfectly fine."

"A few drops you say?" Nanuk took the bottle from Robotbear's paw and looked at it very closely. He sniffed at it and tried to put it on the tip of his muzzle.

"Just take a few drops, and you will see that it will calm you down and you will be pleased with your decision."

"Oh my, everybody is being so smart today!" Nanuk sighed. And he reluctantly opened the vial and took a few drops.

Robotbear watched him anxiously lick up a few drops from the Magic Potion vial.

Nanuk swallowed and said "Are we going to the planet Alas-K, or not?"

Robotbear smiled and said "All right, let's go!"

Faunour had helped Harriet carry the boxes inside the house. There were many more than usual because it was the Christmas special and the bears had caught an incredible number of wishes. They were therefore even more magnificent than the bears at other times of the year.

Harriet smiled at Faunour. "Those are the best bears yet!"

Faunour could only think that these bears might mean that he would never see Harriet again.

"Don't get upset. I will be back," she said, reading his thoughts.

"I hope you will," Faunour said and sighed heavily. He had started to remove one Wish Captor from a Karu's tummy when Robotbear called them.

"All right, then. Departure time! Everybody say farewell to Nanuk. We are on our way."

Faunour, Harriet and the two little polar bear brothers took turns in hugging Nanuk. They all had tears in their eyes, except for Nanuk who suddenly felt light, and brave, and sure of himself.

"Come on, guys, be happy! It is the adventure of a lifetime!" And he bravely climbed into the rocket and sat down by the window. He waved cheerfully at them while Robotbear got into the cockpit next to him.

"Make sure to keep the bottle at hand."

"No worries. I have it right here." Nanuk held on to the Magic Potion tightly and felt the strength it gave him.

The rocket slowly took off to the wondrous planet of bears where soon there would be the first live polar bear.

Nanuk on Alas-K

On the way to Alas-K, Nanuk took a moment to reflect on his life. Perhaps for the last time, he tried to remember his best moments on Earth.

There was the moment he had first seen snow. When he had climbed out of the den he was born in and the first time he went up the hill with his brothers, his mother watching from afar.

Then there was the first time he had tried catching a seal on an ice floe. The seal was sitting there, and Nanuk had tried to approach very carefully, not to alert the seal. He had raised his head slowly out of the ice-cold water, preparing to pounce. At the last moment, the seal must have heard him, diving off and making a quick escape.

Nanuk tried to remember the sensations of the water, the cold, even the hunger. He knew that on Alas-K he would be unable to feel any of those.

Robotbear turned his head slowly toward him, but didn't want to disturb Nanuk's train of thought so he kept

concentrating on the sky. The stars indicated that they were approaching Alas-K. The trip was really not that long. They traveled at the speed of a wish.

"Nanuk, we are here!"

Nanuk was startled.

"Ah. Have we have arrived already?"

This was Alas-K.

Nanuk opened the cockpit door and slowly took the air in.

There was a wonderful smell. Something indescribable floated in the air, something light and sweet.

Nothing could compare to it.

"Welcome to Alas-K, Nanuk. You made it."

"Thank you, Robotbear." Nanuk stretched his limbs. He still felt more or less like his old self.

"When will I start to forget?"

"Actually, Nanuk, it is partly your decision what you forget and what you remember. This planet is a planet of wishes. Everything depends on what you wish for. And never forget that the bear on Alas-K has an ounce of free will."

"I see."

"Take a few deep breaths and enjoy your first impressions. I advise you to go and see Adelaide right away. She will attach your Wish Captor and explain a few things. There is also a small Welcome Party for you afterwards."

Nanuk looked around. And he felt as if he had suddenly no reason to feel anything. A blissful state came over him that was so overpowering that it would have been frightening had there still been a fragment of feeling to account for it.

Adelaide welcomes Nanuk

Enjoying his new enlightened spirit, Nanuk started on his journey. The planet Alas-K was full of colors. The first impressions were of pale blue and different shades of purple. From the landing spot of the rocket, there was a path leading through the Bear Park. When Nanuk looked up to the sky, he saw the bear bubbles full of wishes, but as he didn't know what they were, he mistook them for clouds.

He looked up at the trees, not knowing that Magic Potions were hidden in most of them. They were not the ones that the Knight of the Round Ear had in his cabinet, used for different kinds of travel, but Magic Potions hidden inside the tree trunks that maintained the parallel worlds in harmony. Nobody knew about them, except for the President Teddy Bear and Professor Faufur.

Adelaide was on her way to the Bear Park to meet Nanuk. She was very excited to meet a real polar bear and was going over things to ask him. She wondered how much he still remembered and what he had forgotten already. The paths in the Bear Park formed according to intentions and wishes, and while Adelaide was thinking about Nanuk, the paths rearranged and aligned in such a way that they were walking one towards the other. Nanuk on one side and Adelaide on the other.

Soon, she caught a glimpse of him. She had never seen such a large bear before. Nanuk still had his majestic Earth polar bear appearance and was walking slowly and peacefully, looking up and down, and left and right. But what he saw was impossible to say. On the planet of the bears you could see whatever you wanted to see, and Nanuk did not know that yet, so he was looking at undefined trees and shrubs and flowers that seemed to be in an unstable state, caught in a flicker.

Nanuk used this liberating feeling of emptiness for a complete new start. He looked at the surrounding elements and when he looked through them, he was reminded of places he had loved through the things he was looking at now. There was a haze and sometimes, beneath the clouds of undefined trees and sky, he would catch a glimpse of what he wanted most. He was where he wanted to be.

The only decision that he made was that he would be waiting for a miracle. He would walk around in this park and enjoy waiting for something. At that moment, Adelaide called out to him.

"Nanuk! Welcome to the planet Alas-K!"

"Hello there. Are you Adelaide?"

"Yes, I am. I am so glad you are here."

"Thank you, Adelaide. I am here now indeed. And what a wonderful place it is."

"Oh, please, we need to hurry. I have to attach your Wish Captor to your tummy before you make any decisions. Otherwise you might develop more free will than you ought to, and around here this could make things very hard for you."

Nanuk was content. He had anticipated that his free will might be impaired by the Wish Captor. He hoped the beauty of that moment in the park would remain with him for the whole time he would be on the planet.

Adelaide took Nanuk by the paw and they quickly made their way to the Nuzzle Studio.

"Come on in, Nanuk," Adelaide invited him. "This is where I attach the Wish Captors to the new bears and I also touch up muzzles and ears from time to time, when the wishes are not precise enough."

Nanuk sat down and waited. He looked around and noticed the sketches of the Nuzzle positions.

"Am I going to learn how to do the Nuzzle, too?"

"I certainly hope so. The Knight of the Round Ear and I have already enlisted you for the next training season. You will also be watching the bears on Earth at the Telescope Park."

While Adelaide chose the right Wish Captor in the box, Nanuk asked:

"When I will watch the bears on Earth, will I remember that I used to be one of them?"

"Nanuk, I have found your Wish Captor. It is a special one, as it concerns your being. Usually, the Wish Captor catches bear wishes that concern features, but yours must make you into an Alas-K bear, as you are already fully formed."

"Most of all I need to learn the Nuzzle."

"Yes, indeed, this will help you become a bear of this planet. But you should still watch the shape of the bears on Earth."

"I am not so sure, Adelaide. I am sorry to contradict you, but I think I should watch the bears on this planet if I want to become one of you."

Adelaide put one paw under her muzzle and took a pause to think. "You are probably right, Nanuk. It does seem more important that you watch the bears right here."

Nanuk smiled. "You can attach the Wish Captor now. I am ready to let go of my old life. Let's make a new, fresh and totally clean slate for a new start!"

"All right!" Adelaide cheered. "Here you go."

And she carefully attached the new Wish Captor to Nanuk's belly.

"Bears are us"

"Welcome everybody on the planet Alas-K and elsewhere in the Imagination! Squeak!"

Bearmouse always started his afternoon show in this manner. On the time slot called 'Stuff about bears' he presented a program named 'Chit chat for little bears.'

The special occasion of having a real Earth polar bear on the planet called for a special edition of 'Bears are us' where Bearmouse explained life on the bear planet. He also offered insights on important details about the bears on Earth. And with Nanuk as his guest, he was very pleased to finally get a first-hand view on life on Earth.

As the Journalist-Philosopher on Alas-K, his was the responsibility to keep the Alas-K bears up to date on current events. He looked quite a bit like a mouse and started most of his sentences with 'Squeak!'

Hector and Big Creamy were among the very few who faithfully watched his program. Even if Bearmouse was respected for his knowledge and general insight, the other bears lacked the patience to watch his show because it could become quite complicated. But Hector, the Bear Image Secretary, and Big Creamy, the Secretary of Puzzlement, were assiduous viewers. They not only needed to keep up with bear facts, but they also enjoyed being amazed, and sometimes even confused.

"Come on, it's time," Big Creamy said when he collected Hector at his desk. "Let's go to the Television room. I hope we aren't the only ones watching Bearmouse's show, you know how angry he can get. Oh! Oh!"

Hector agreed, "You are right. Especially Little Creamy who should be here to watch the show with us. Bearmouse is always so worried that Little Creamy misses his show, but as this is his first day as the planet's EMOT, Bearmouse will certainly understand if he is not here with us now."

"Oh well, you know Bearmouse. He has a temper."

"That is true," Hector said and smiled knowingly.

Indeed, Bearmouse was known for his sudden angry fits. He would walk out of the room, slamming doors, his pointy muzzle up in the air and his arms folded tightly in front of his chest.

Big Creamy and Hector went to the Television room. Hector opened the door, and they were once again the only ones watching Bearmouse's show.

On Alas-K, the technical equipment was at the cutting edge of technology. The bears could enjoy telescopes, rockets and television screens that were among the best available in the parallel worlds. On Alas-K everything was created by wishes and the technical equipment would adjust accordingly to any situation that presented itself.

Hector and Big Creamy made themselves comfortable in the big Television Room. Hector had brought some honey lemonade. "Mmmm. Hoimsli!" murmured Big Creamy. Hoimsli was the word that described something extremely tasty.

"Squeak!" said Bearmouse. "Today, I will explain how a bear is shaped. You all know that we are shaped according to wishes that are sent to us from planet Earth."

Bearmouse looked around.

"Most of the time, children wish for bears, but some adults who cannot let go of their love for teddy bears send us their wishes, too. In order to become perfectly shaped teddy bears, Adelaide, the Nuzzling Supervisor of the Bear

Workshop, attaches small screens to our tummies that catch the wishes. These screens are called Wish Captors."

Hector looked at Big Creamy and asked: "Wish Captors? Do you have one of those?"

"Well ...," said Big Creamy looking down his big belly. "I don't see one, actually."

"Well, good. Me neither," replied Hector, feeling reassured, tucking in his chin and feeling his tummy with his paw for a screen with little stars on it.

"Squeak! Dear viewers on the planet Alas-K, planet of the bears, you must know that not everyone has a Wish Captor. Only bears who are newly arrived on the planet get one. I will come to this in a moment. But now please welcome Nanuk, a polar bear who has recently arrived on our planet having left planet Earth to escape a climate change. Please, give Nanuk a round of applause."

The audience applauded, a sliding door opened and Nanuk stepped on stage. As a former polar bear, Nanuk already had the perfect bear shape, but he was much bigger than Bearmouse. His size had not yet adjusted to the Alas-K bear size. When they arrive on the bear planet, real Earth bears need to catch a certain number of teddy bear wishes before they become a little smaller.

"Welcome, Nanuk," said Bearmouse, reaching for Nanuk's paw to greet him. "Please sit down and say hello to our audience."

Nanuk shook Bearmouse's paw and sat down gingerly in the guest chair. It was a bit small for him. The chair had not yet had time to adjust to the big bear's size. But it started stretching immediately as soon as Nanuk sat down. He smiled and said "Hello, bears!"

"The planet Alas-K is the planet of bears, as you know. And you, you are a bear!"

"Yes, I certainly am," said Nanuk.

"But, I would like to know if you were created by a wish," Bearmouse asked.

"Well," said Nanuk. "I don't know, actually. I don't remember."

"Ah! You have lost your memory, like all Alas-K bears. You are one of us now. Excellent!"

"Is that a good thing?" Nanuk tilted his head.

"Of course it is. When you lose your memory, you can become a perfect bear for a child on Earth, you see."

"I see," said Nanuk who didn't see much, in fact.

"Let me explain. Only a bear that doesn't remember anything can change according to wishes, as he needs to be freed from any previous state of his own choosing that would attach him to his past, do you understand?"

"Well, I'm not sure," said Nanuk.

"Bears on the planet Alas-K are of three kinds," said Bearmouse who explained the same bear facts in his show every time.

"There are for one the old teddy bears who had to leave Earth after their child had grown too big to play with them. Those bears have been rescued by the Abandoned Bear Rescue Squad. The other kind, the most common on this planet, are the bears who are spontaneously created by Imagination. And now, there is a new kind: real bears from Earth who have escaped some kind of distress."

"Well, I might indeed have come from another planet. I think I remember a rocket, vaguely," said Nanuk, now rubbing his head with his paw and testing the limits of his poor memory.

"Yes, our rocket that usually brings Alas-K bears to planet Earth, now also brings back bears from Earth. Do you remember Robotbear? He is the pilot of the rocket and has a special quality that protects him against the atmosphere on Earth."

"Robotbear? Why? What is wrong with the atmosphere on Earth?"

Nanuk became frightened and realized that he had come to a very strange place. He was about to regret his former life as an Earth polar bear, when his memory cleared up, and he could not remember the reason why he had been so scared. And so, he stopped being scared right away.

He took a deep breath, and relaxed in the chair that now was the appropriate size for him.

"Ah, the atmosphere. Well, for the Alas-K bear, the trip to Earth is a big change. He is about to leave the planet of bears to become a teddy bear and, when he arrives on Earth, he becomes a toy and falls asleep." Bearmouse explained.

The audience held their breath. The bears fall asleep! That was a frightening bit of information.

"Squeak! No need to worry, dear bears," said Bearmouse, looking at Nanuk who had not said a word.

"Nanuk? Are you ok? You knew that becoming a teddy bear was the main purpose of the Alas-K bear, didn't you?"

Nanuk nervously rubbed his paw on his nose.

"Well, you know, Bearmouse, I have come here, to the planet of bears, hoping for a better life. On Earth, seals have become rare, and I have spent endless weeks looking for food on very cold ice," said Nanuk, suddenly remembering bits and pieces from his previous life.

He shivered a little, once the memory flash came back to him. "I was looking forward to being here on Alas-K, where bears are carefree and happy, and need not worry about survival. At least, that's what I understood from Faunour, but now, I learn that there are wishes that call us back to Earth in order to become teddy bears. How dreadful!"

"Dreadful? Well, that's a first!" Bearmouse was quite surprised, as he had never interviewed a bear before who did not wish to become a teddy bear. "Yes, it is true that the bear on Alas-K has certain obligations. He must constantly watch the bears on Earth, and he depends on his Wish Captor. Especially the bear who is new to the planet."

But of course, Nanuk was the first real Earth bear to arrive on the planet and who might one day return to Earth as a teddy bear.

"You see, this is exactly what I mean, I'll have to go back to Earth." Nanuk put his paws on his muzzle and sighed.

"Yes, one day, but we don't know how quickly a former Earth bear can become a teddy bear. Let me see your Wish Captor."

Nanuk stretched a little, and indeed, on his tummy, underneath his white fur, appeared a small screen with stars.

"Oh, Nanuk, good job! You have already caught a few wishes. The first three stars are already showing some color."

And indeed, when Nanuk looked down at his Wish Captor, he saw the slightly colored stars and sighed. He understood that his time on the planet was already limited and his face wore a worried expression again.

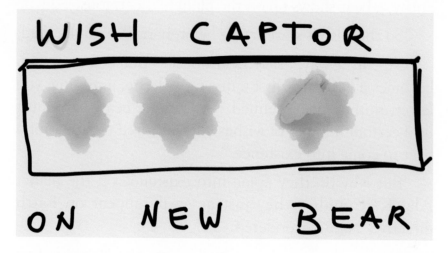

"Please Nanuk, don't worry. To become a teddy bear for the children on Earth is the main purpose of the Alas-K bear's existence."

"Oh dear," said Nanuk.

"But we have only had experience with spontaneously created bears until now." Bearmouse added quickly.

"Really? How do those bears arrive on the planet?" Nanuk asked with sudden interest.

"Well, this is a complicated matter that we don't really understand. But sometimes, when we walk through the Bear

Park, a new bear appears in front of us. Out of the blue, so to speak."

"Fascinating. I shall go for a stroll in the Bear Park later. I wish I could see bears appear like that," Nanuk said, feeling happier. Also, as his short time memory had faded, he had begun to forget that he was to become a teddy bear.

"It happens all the time, actually. Wishes are very powerful and once they have come together to create an entity, a bear shows up on the planet," Bearmouse added.

"So the wishes start acting beforehand?" Nanuk asked.

"Yes, in a way," said Bearmouse. "But before a wish becomes a wish, it is first a dream, a desire, a musing, you know, nothing very defined. To create a bear there must be a certain number of wishes concentrated together for a bear to come into existence."

"But why do they come into existence on the planet Alas-K? Couldn't they just as easily appear on Earth directly?" Nanuk wondered.

"No, the bear that materializes on our planet is first only a possibility. He becomes an actual bear with well-defined round ears and a pointy muzzle and the recognizable bear shape when the wishes are precise enough. Do you understand?"

"Well, I can't say that I do. The incoming wishes make the bear a bear, so to speak?"

"Yes. The more wishes a bear catches, the more enhanced his features become, and that's how the bear evolves."

"So it is more like a process then? Does the success depend on the number of wishes captured?"

"In a way, yes. If many children wish for a bear, he gets a better color, a better shape because his existence is more wanted, therefore he is stronger, and his passage from possibility to reality is easier."

"Oh. So, if many children wish for a bear together, the bear forms more quickly?"

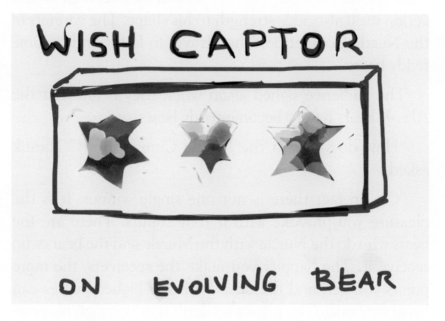

"Yes! If they can focus on the same wish, it happens even faster."

"Oh, that is very interesting," Nanuk said.

The audience on the other hand had started yawning, and a few bears were snoring.

Bearmouse was used to his audience falling asleep the moment information became more complicated, so he didn't worry about it too much.

"Yes, the wishes gather on the Wish Captor and more and more the colors become sharper and the bear becomes an entity that can do the Nuzzle with the Muzzle and travel to Earth!"

"A bear can be more or less of a bear?"

"There is something like a threshold. Once the bear has enough stability to become an entity, he can learn the Nuzzle with the Muzzle which makes him more stable, because the action itself also adds strength to his shape. The winners of the Nuzzle Competition then travel to Earth and become teddy bears."

The audience sighed again when they heard that the Alas-K bears had to become teddy bears.

"How do you win the Nuzzle Competition?" Nanuk asked.

"Oh, in fact there is not one single winner. It is the pleasure you provoke with it that counts. There are the bears who do the Nuzzle with the Muzzle and the bears who receive it. The happier you make the receivers, the more points you get, and the bears with the highest scores can leave for Earth. The ones who don't score enough pleasure points have to reenlist with Adelaide and the Knight of the Round Ear for more training, and will leave the following month."

"Pleasure points for the Nuzzle with the Muzzle. Mmm Hmmm," Nanuk said, and started to think that maybe the whole teddy bear thing was not that dreadful after all.

"But still, Bearmouse, there is one thing that I don't understand. Why do we have to watch the bears on Earth?"

At that moment, Hector looked at Big Creamy and said "Yes, why do we do that? Indeed, I wonder."

"I have always wondered about that myself, but you know, I am, after all, the Secretary of Puzzlement whose business it is to be astonished, so it is quite normal for me to be puzzled and wonder about things."

"Yes, it is puzzling, indeed," said Hector, as he leaned back in his chair, took a sip of lemonade and concentrated again on what Bearmouse was saying.

"Squeak! Why do we watch the bears on Earth? Very simple. It is only by watching the bears on Earth and the way they move that we can get our typical bear shape. It is not enough to catch the wishes, as they are solely about the features of the bear: namely the pointy muzzle and the round ears. In order to become the perfect bear shape, we need to know what bears look like, how they move and how they behave. That way, each property knows how to go to the right place, and the stars on the Wish Captor get a better outline."

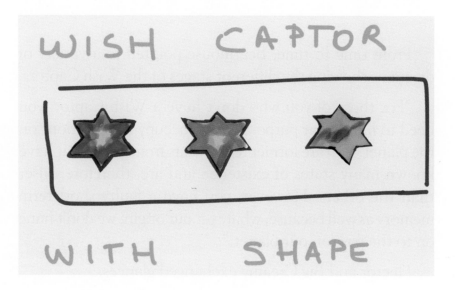

To sum up: first there is the idea of a bear. Then there is a pure form that comes to the planet, and then, all the wishes come together to create the perfect bear. And once the Wish Captors are full, the bear is stable enough to become a teddy bear on Earth. It's all very simple really."

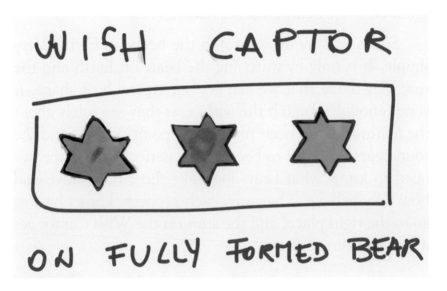

From time to time, Bearmouse pointed to a variety of diagrams showing the different stages of the Wish Captors.

"For those of you who don't have a Wish Captor, you need to fulfill your purpose as you occupy key positions on the planet. You are former teddy bears from Earth that have known many states of existence and are, therefore, wiser than the others. However, you have a faulty short-term memory as well because, whatever our origin, we don't hang on to the past on our planet."

Hector and Big Creamy exchanged glances.

"In order not to confuse you too much, I will leave off here for today and talk to you all tomorrow. If you have any questions about bear facts, please leave a message on my board.

One fact for today: to answer last week's question about ears, the Asian black bear has the largest ears of all bears.

Nanuk, enjoy yourself on the planet. Everything will be fine, no need to worry. You'll figure everything out. And have fun watching us, as you will need to know how we move here on the planet in order to become one of us. Goodbye for now, dear fellow bears. And don't forget, we don't remember anything!"

Bearmouse noted the worried expression disappear from Nanuk's face, and he also saw a few lights blinking on the keyboard in front of him. One was the sign that Teddy Bear himself, the President, wanted to talk to him, but it was the other light that concerned him a little more. Adelaide had sent him a message of distress, which must mean that there was a problem at the Bear Workshop.

Perhaps there was something wrong with the bears' shapes according to the Wish Captors?

There were only two things that mattered on the planet and they were the Nuzzle with the Muzzle and the general look of the bears.

"Bears don't have stripes"

Recently, Little Creamy had been promoted from Observer-in-Chief to Engineer at the Maintenance of Telescopes, or EMOT.

As always, Little Creamy carried his huge screwdriver that was way too big for him. Little Creamy was a little nervous about his new job and dropped his screwdriver a lot.

"Oh dear, what's the matter with this thing?"

The screwdriver had once again slipped from his paws, perhaps because of his nervousness or simply because the screwdriver was just far too big for such a little bear.

"Do you see?" a voice called out, suddenly.

"Mmm Hmmm," Little Creamy said, as he usually did. "Do I see what?" He responded calmly, not at all wondering where the voice may have come from.

"The bears! You can see very well that they don't look the same."

"They don't look the same, you say. The same as what?"

"I don't think there is anything wrong with us. It's the bears, they don't look the same," the telescope repeated.

"What are you talking about, Telescope?" Little Creamy said, understanding that it was the telescope's voice.

"Let me see." He looked through the eyepiece once more. "I can't see any bears."

He tapped a little on the top of the eyepiece.

"Hey, what do you think I am? A broken refrigerator?"

Little Creamy was not sure he knew what a refrigerator was, but was afraid to ask and to appear stupid.

"No, of course not. But what are you showing me, Telescope? Those are not the bears we usually see."

"This is what I am trying to tell you. The bears don't look the same."

"But, Telescope, this is definitely not even a bear. It has stripes."

"True," the Telescope conceded. It had to admit that it had never seen a bear with stripes before.

"But it has a pointy muzzle, almost roundish ears, and a very long neck."

"Look at its head. It is wearing a funny hat."

And indeed, the animal had stripes and was wearing something on its head that looked like a funnel.

"Oh, hello, Little Creamy! What's going on here?" Hazelnut had just arrived at that moment and interrupted the conversation with the Telescope in a most impolite manner.

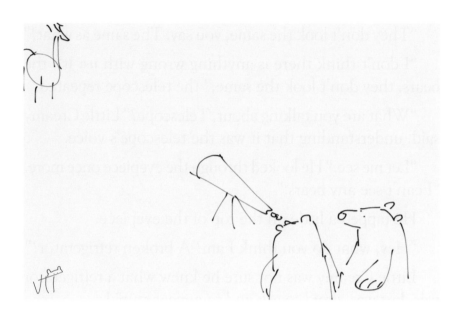

The Telescope stopped conversing immediately with Little Creamy the moment he noticed Hazelnut.

"Oh, hello Hazelnut, there you are. I began my check on the bears this morning, and look what I saw."

Hazelnut put his nose close to the eyepiece and blinked. He adjusted the focus and zoomed in on a magnificent brown bear raising its paw to catch a salmon in a river on the planet Earth.

"Yes, so? I see a perfect specimen of a grizzly bear catching a fish. What is so surprising about that?"

"What? Let me see," Little Creamy said, a little alarmed. When he put his eye to the eyepiece and had a closer look, he saw the grizzly bear as well, and rubbed his paw under his chin, saying "Mmm Hmmm" a few times in a row.

Hazelnut shook his head in a superior manner and said "Let's get to work now. Everybody is here and we will start watching the bears on Earth. You are to take screen captures every fifteen minutes and write down every detail you notice. There is a little beep to remind you to push the button. Please pay close attention. We will then make flipbooks, so that we can trace any changes in the image of the bear."

Little Creamy stared at Hazelnut who had taken charge and said "Mmm Hmmm," once more.

All the other bears looked up from their telescopes and stared at Little Creamy. They didn't know if they should take orders from Hazelnut.

"Yes, yes, go ahead and do that. Get to work, bears." The bears all resumed their positions in front of the telescopes and pushed buttons to take screen captures of the bears they watched on Earth. Most of the bears were catching salmon.

Once Little Creamy was by himself in front of the telescope, he checked again, and for the rest of the afternoon, he only saw perfectly shaped grizzly bears catching salmon in a river on the planet Earth.

And the telescope did not speak to him again for the rest of the day.

Nanuk meets the Kitchen Giraffe

Little Creamy switched off his screen and said "Mmm Hmm." He had just watched Bearmouse's show on tape, because he had to be present all day at the bear watch session. He had, therefore, missed the meeting with Hector and Big Creamy.

Although Bearmouse was his best friend, Bearmouse would not speak to him for weeks if Little Creamy missed one of his shows.

Even though the concept of weeks was not something that concerned the Alas-K bears and their memory was focused on a moment-to-moment perception only, so the passing of time did not really trouble them.

Alas-K bears have no short-term memory and they live more or less in the present, but they are constantly afraid to appear stupid, as they don't remember what just happened. Or have I said that already?

"The Wish Captors catch wishes and create the shape of the bear, little by little."

Mmm Hmmm.

Little Creamy tried to hang on to this information for as long as he could. And he looked down on his own belly, noticing that there was no Wish Captor. Yes, he was a former teddy bear, too, and therefore not subjected to a time limitation on the planet Alas-K. He tucked his huge screwdriver under his arm and went to see the telescopes.

It was the following day.

"Ah! Little Creamy!"

The telescope had been waiting for him impatiently and immediately greeted him when he arrived. It was the telescope that had shown him the strange animal with stripes and a funnel on its head. Little Creamy didn't know who had spoken to him as he had forgotten the whole incident already, so he went about his business as if nothing had happened.

"Hey! Creamy!" repeated the telescope.

Little Creamy looked around, not seeing anyone. He adjusted the focus on the telescope and put his eye closer to the eyepiece.

"Creamy! Can you see it now?" The telescope asked.

Little Creamy tilted his head first to the left and then to the right.

"Telescope? Is that you?"

"Of course it's me. Look at the animal now."

Little Creamy looked closer and saw an animal with stripes.

"This is not a bear," he said, matter-of-factly.

"Indeed!" said the telescope.

"Mmm Hmmm," said Little Creamy.

"What can it be?" The telescope said and added "And also, where can it be? It doesn't seem to me that it is on Earth."

Little Creamy tried to juggle his screwdriver under his arm without dropping it and zoomed in on the animal. It had a long thin neck, very long eyelashes and black and white stripes. A blue funnel sat on its head. It looked around in a ladylike manner.

And when Little Creamy followed its gaze with the telescope, he saw something even more astonishing, another non-bear!

"Telescope, what is that?" And the telescope zoomed in on the other animal that was obviously not a bear either.

"It has a long muzzle, but pointy ears and a long white stripe on its muzzle."

"Indeed."

"But wait, there is yet another one!" And the telescope zoomed in on a short but long animal with a very strange tail.

"I wonder who these creatures are? They appear to be standing right in the middle of the Bear Park."

"Yes, Telescope, you are right. See, there is Nanuk!"

Nanuk was indeed lumbering around in the Bear Park. His eyes wide open, his head turning in all directions. He didn't want to miss the phenomenon of a spontaneous bear creation.

His memory was fading quickly, so he had written down what Bearmouse had told him.

He wanted to remember that bears appear on the planet out of thin air.

The other thing he didn't want to remember didn't bother him.

When he learned that bears on the planet lose their memory, he immediately thought that this could be a good thing and might keep him from being sad.

He didn't want to remember that there was a screen at the bottom of his tummy that caught wishes and might one day call him back to Earth.

However, he did want to remember that bears appeared spontaneously in the middle of the Bear Park, and had written that information down.

Here he was now, walking happily through the park, where the trees were green, the paths were grey, and the sky was blue. The Bear Park looked more or less like a park on Earth, with trees lining paths, and flowers growing here and there.

Suddenly, Nanuk stopped and gaped. Right there, in front of him there was a peculiar animal with a very long neck and black and white stripes. His memory was fading, but he was still able to recognize beyond any doubt that this animal was clearly not a bear.

"Oh, well, hello there!" The animal said, and batted her eyelashes.

"Hello," Nanuk said, looking rather disappointed. He expected to see a spontaneous bear creation, but instead, there he was, facing a creature that was very different from any other kind he had ever seen or at least this was how it felt. Nanuk did not remember exactly what kind of other creatures he had seen before.

"Hello! How are you?" asked the animal, batting her

eyelashes again, and inclining her head. She was quite a bit taller than Nanuk on account of her long neck and legs.

"I am fine, thank you," said Nanuk. "And, how are you? ...And if you don't mind me asking, who are you?" He added.

"Very well, thank you. I am the Kitchen Giraffe, you see. And who are you?"

"I am Nanuk, a bear."

"Of course you are a bear, dear. This is after all the planet of bears."

"Well..." Nanuk hesitated to state the obvious. "You, on the other hand..."

"Yes, yes, I know what you are going to say. I am not a bear. I know that. Thank you very much." The Kitchen Giraffe looked a little vexed and turned her head in the other direction, as if she wanted to hide tears.

Nanuk frowned. "Forgive me, Kitchen Giraffe. Please, I don't mean to offend you, but you see, I was told that here in the Bear Park, bears appear spontaneously, out of nothing so to speak. Therefore, you must understand my bewilderment when I saw you here... But let me add, you have a very lovely hat."

"Thank you," said the Kitchen Giraffe, turning her head slowly back toward Nanuk. She liked compliments. "I am here because of a confusion, you see."

"A confusion?" said Nanuk, starting to feel rather confused himself.

"Yes. The image became confused. Mixed up, if you will. Something about the properties, you see."

"What properties?"

"Bears are created by wishes, you see." The Kitchen Giraffe started, and Nanuk suddenly remembered what he had been trying to forget.

"Yes, the wishes, of course," Nanuk said, feeling a little upset again.

"The wishes are about properties, you see. A pointy nose and rounded ears mostly, for bears. But someone wants to change that. The planet needs other animals, you see, so there are more properties now. Stripes, and long necks, and so on, you see."

Nanuk looked at the Kitchen Giraffe, wondering a little why she kept repeating "you see" and said "You certainly know a lot about these things. Do you have a Wish Captor too?"

"I am not sure. Isn't the Wish Captor for bears only? Adelaide is in charge of that."

"Adelaide? When did you arrive here? How do you know so much about the planet?"

"I arrived yesterday. The passing of time is difficult to understand here, you see. But I think it was during the last bear observation session."

Indeed, the days on the Planet Alas-K were measured by the telescope observation sessions of the bears on Earth. "Adelaide tried to catch us."

"Us? You mean there are more animals that are not bears here on the planet?" Nanuk asked, becoming more and more disappointed. His hope to see a spontaneous bear creation was beginning to vanish.

"Weeheehee!" someone said behind them, all of a sudden.

"What is wrong with the Wish Captors?"

Adelaide was pacing nervously around her workshop, waiting for Bearmouse to arrive.

Adelaide was very concerned. She was monitoring the bears for their perfect bear shape and wanted to verify the good functioning of the screens, the receptiveness to wishes and the general appearance of each star.

As an Alas-K bear, Adelaide also had a very faulty memory and needed help in keeping track of events. To help her remember, she had posted on the walls of her office many different flipbooks explaining the evolution of the Wish Captors over time. They showed that the stars on the Wish Captors were first translucent, and then, little by little, filled up with more and more color with each incoming wish. When the stars were bright enough and the bear shape was close enough to the perfect bear shape, then the bear could learn how to do the Nuzzle with the Muzzle and participate in the Nuzzle Competition at the Bear Festival, before being sent to Earth.

Adelaide's workshop was full of sketches showing pointy bear muzzles and Nuzzle with the Muzzle poses. Those sketches showed how to position the muzzle on the child's cheek in order to do the Nuzzle with the Muzzle correctly. Every month, the selected bears came to Adelaide for special training that allowed them to become a beloved teddy bear for a child on Earth. But today, everything was different.

Usually, the bear shape was perfect, the muzzle was pointy and the ears were rounded and most importantly, the bears were bears. However recently, Adelaide had spotted a few very strange looking animals in the Bear Park who didn't look like bears at all. Bears had neither stripes nor long thin necks; neither did they wear a funnel on their head nor did they say "wheeheehee." She was at a loss, and hoped Bearmouse would know what to do.

"Squeak," Bearmouse said, entering the workshop, a little out of breath. "What's going on, Adelaide?"

"At last, Bearmouse! I am so glad you are here. I need your help. Please tell me what is happening to the Wish Captors! Look!"

Bearmouse looked at the screens and inspected them carefully. Indeed, the Wish Captors were not working properly.

Usually, each Wish Captor had a certain number of stars, and each star filled up more and more with color with each incoming wish. Each Wish Captor had the same properties assigned to each star. The first one concerned the muzzle, the second the ears, the third the particular bear shape, the fourth the texture.

All the symbols on the Wish Captors were stars, and all the properties on the Wish Captors were about bears. Adelaide usually checked them before attaching them on a new bear. But now, it looked like new symbols had appeared, as well as new properties. Bearmouse had a little more memory than the other inhabitants of the planet, so he needed less help with flipbooks. He remembered on his own that the symbols on the Wish Captors were usually stars.

"Squeak! There is a half-moon symbol, and a heart, and a sun, and the properties are "stripes", "long neck" and "a white streak on the nose." Interesting! What has happened to the Wish Captors?" Bearmouse inspected the new symbols, and when he touched them, they lit up a little. He could swipe his paw on the screen to switch from one property to the next. The key bear features like "rounded ears" and "pointy muzzle" were no longer the only properties caught by the Wish Captors.

Bearmouse had a sudden flash of intuition.

"Adelaide, have you spoken to Faunour recently? I suspect he has a paw in this pie!"

"Bear up! It's our invention!"

Faunour was working hard. With Harriet gone home for Christmas, he had more time to develop his invention.

He had locked himself up in his office and was looking through the eye-piece of his self-invented machine, mumbling to himself. "Stripes … check, long ears … check, tail in shape of a fir tree … check…" Then he pushed a few buttons and took some notes in a notebook.

Removing the Wish Captors from the arriving bears he had developed some knowledge of engineering. For some time now, Faunour was concerned for his fellow bears who could not play and talk and make their own decisions anymore, the way they had done on their planet, once they had made it to Earth.

So, he asked himself, why should bears be the only plush animals that children wish for? Many other kinds of animals existed and could make them just as happy as a bear did, or so Faunour thought.

Faunour was not aware of the importance of the Nuzzle with the Muzzle, nor did he know that the helpless state of the teddy bear was necessary to spread love.

"Bear up!" He said to himself.

Bear up! was the motto of his revolutionary movement, the movement for the liberation of bears, or MOLOB, for short. Faunour wanted to save Earth Bears from distress, yet he wanted to protect his fellow Alas-K bears from their fate as lifeless teddy bears. These two wishes came into conflict when the Earth bears on Alas-K had enough wishes on their Wish Captors to participate in the Nuzzle Race and risk winning the competition and return to Earth as a teddy bear.

The least Faunour could do was try to prevent them from becoming teddy bears too quickly, or even change the outcome of the wishes. Therefore, he had invented an ingenious machine that would create new animals on the planet of the bears. His machine could reprogram the Wish Captor by opening it up to other properties that were not the ones associated with bears. By manipulating the properties programmed on the Wish Captors, Faunour had discovered that he could bring new animals into existence. The Alas-K bear was after all created by wishes so why not open the Wish Captors to new wishes and, thereby, open the planet to new animals?

Animals that appear on the planet of the bears are at first not quite stable enough to come into existence without a Wish Captor attached, this enables them to become fully formed animals that can travel to Earth and become plush animals.

Faunour was of course aware of the fact that this invention of his might cause quite a stir among his fellow bears up there on the planet, and he was nervous. He was expecting an emergency call any minute. He tried to keep busy with his work so that his worries wouldn't catch up with him.

The one thing that Faunour had not taken into account was the special quality of the teddy bear that is to be the only animal capable of performing the Nuzzle with the Muzzle properly. Faunour had never experienced the Nuzzle with the Muzzle himself because he was a spontaneous bear creation and he had been banned from the planet and sent to Earth without ever becoming a beloved bear for a child.

After all, Faunour still had his Wish Captor attached to his tummy, he therefore didn't understand the secret power of the Nuzzle nor the bliss that it provided.

Any new animal arriving on the planet of bears would have to learn the Nuzzle with the Muzzle just as well as the bears in order to compete in the Nuzzle Competition held every month at the Bear Festival. This was the only way to select the bears who were ready to go to Earth. Any animal that was not a bear must have an appropriate muzzle that could be rubbed on the child's cheek in order to become a plush animal. Some properties actually were universal, for example, "descending from the forehead in a straight line" applied to most muzzles on most animals and could, therefore, be used as a basic requirement for the Nuzzle with the Muzzle.

Faunour programmed a number of new properties into the Wish Captor programming device. But when he put in "green almond eyes" and "off-white stripes and ginger stripes," Tigah popped up in front of him.

"Hello there," said Faunour, not sounding too surprised - a habit he had picked up when he was still living on the planet. As the Alas-K bear had a very poor memory, he was quite vain, and was constantly trying not to appear dumb.

"Meow," Tigah said.

"Well, meow to you, too," Faunour said cheerfully. "Who are you?"

"So, you create bears, right?" Tigah tapped one paw on Faunour's shoulder in an accusing manner and came straight to the point.

"Well, not exactly. Wishes create bears, but again… who are you?"

"Oh, forgive me. I am Tigah! A cat!"

"Yes, you are a cat. I can see that. But what are you doing here? And how did you get here?"

"Well, let's not get ahead of ourselves. I will tell you exactly why I am here. Just give me a minute!"

Tigah replied, carefully enunciating his words and stroking his whiskers, he looked at Faunour inquisitively. He slowly swallowed the last crumbs of the blueberry pie.

"I am here thanks to the famous blueberry pies the Famous Wood Hound bakes in the Forest of the Same Name. You should know that, bear!"

Faunour began to feel a little uneasy but tried to appear outwardly cool and in control of the situation. Also, he was wondering if the name of the Forest was "Wood Hound" or "blueberry pies."

"Of course, of course, the Famous Wood Hound and his blueberry pies, everyone knows about those," Faunour said, waving his paw, although he did not have the faintest idea what Tigah was talking about.

"Come on, quit pretending! I know that you bears never understand anything. Must be your memory! Ha!" Tigah said and circled Faunour, threateningly.

Faunour frowned and tried not to be offended. He decided to cross his arms and wait, and not say another word before he knew the whole story.

Tigah circled Faunour a few more times, looking around. "You have reprogrammed the Wish Captors, I hear. New animals on the planet of bears, huh? What an idea!"

"Emm…"

"Yes? Do you want to say something, bear?" Tigah asked, raising his nose.

"No, no, please Tigah, continue."

"You want other animals on the planet of bears so that you are not the only ones who become mindless and dumb, is that right?"

"Well, that is a little harsh. I would not say dumb. Numb might be a better word."

"All right, whatever. Numb. But still, you know that they will have to do the Nuzzle with the Muzzle, as you call it. Nuzzle with the Muzzle! Ha!"

Faunour had been dreading a call from Adelaide, but now he began to wish for it.

"Well, …yes… I guess so. Do you have a problem with that?"

"Meooow!" Tigah yowled, raising his voice. "Do I have a problem with that, you ask? I certainly do, bear."

"And why is that?" Faunour asked, timidly.

"I will tell you why, bear! The Nuzzle with the Muzzle is not your invention, it is ours!" Tigah said, putting both his front paws on the table making no noise at all as his paws were particularly soft.

"It is?" Faunour could not hide his surprise this time.

"Of course it is, bear. We have been rubbing our noses on people's legs for ages!"

"Sure, sure, of course you have," said Faunour. "On their legs." He added, lowering his voice.

"Yes, the legs, the cheeks, whatever! Important is the rubbing, isn't it? The technique!" Tigah said, carefully enunciating the words again. "I will see you around, bear. I will leave now, and you can figure out what to do with that information!"

Tigah disappeared as suddenly as he had appeared, and Faunour sank back in his chair with a sigh of relief.

Meanwhile, Adelaide and Bearmouse had set up the interplanetary communication screen in order to call Faunour. It rang a few times before he answered.

"Hello, planet Alas-K! What's up?" Faunour said, trying to sound as upbeat as possible.

"Hi, Faunour! What's new with you?" Adelaide said.

"Well, not much. I just had a very strange visitor."

"Was it a bear?" Bearmouse asked.

"No, not a bear."

"Ah, we have a lot of non-bear visitors here as well! Do you know why, by any chance?"

"Me? Why would I know anything about that?"

"Well, the Wish Captors show many new properties, and we were wondering if, somehow, you had anything to do with that?"

"Many new properties you say? Interesting."

"Come on, Faunour! Have you been messing with the Wish Captors?" Adelaide said, impatiently.

Faunour did not know how to get out of this question. "Well, you know our memory is not so good, I don't remember exactly."

"You can tell us. We know you want to open the planet to other animals, and we know that you know that it causes us trouble. Teddy Bear will be so angry!"

Faunour wanted to know if his plan had worked, and if the programming of new properties had already created new animals on the planet. Adelaide had mentioned non-bears. That sounded promising.

"What did you mean you have non-bear visitors too?"

Adelaide looked at Bearmouse. And Bearmouse said "Squeak! Yes, indeed, Adelaide spotted a number of strange animals in the Bear Park the other day!"

Faunour felt a little jolt of happiness. "Really? Who are they?"

"Oh, we haven't met them. They escaped."

"Where did they go?"

"I don't know. I saw black and white stripes, a long thin neck, and I heard 'Wheeeheehee!' and then they were gone," Adelaide said.

"You have to find them," Faunour said. "It is extraordinary. Non-bears on the planet of the bears."

"Squeak! I am sure you are responsible for this," Bearmouse said.

Faunour said "I am very busy right now, maybe we can talk about this later? Please try to find the new animals. It's very important! You will soon understand why."

"All right. We will talk to you later. Bye for now." Adelaide said and switched off the screen. She turned to Bearmouse and said "Come on, let's go and find the non-bears."

Bearmouse and Adelaide find the non-bears

The Kitchen Giraffe tried to nibble on a nearby tree but spat out the leaves immediately. "This does not taste like anything, you see."

"Wheeeheeehee!" said the Appropriate Horse. "Those trees are imaginary! What did you think they would taste like? Bears on planet Alas-K only eat imaginary things. They don't know what taste is."

"You seem to know a lot about this planet," said the Famous Wood Hound. "My blueberry pies taste very Hoimsli. That's what Tigah said." Turning to the Kitchen Giraffe, he added "Why should imaginary trees not have taste? Try again! Maybe you have to imagine the taste."

The Kitchen Giraffe said "mm" and tried to tug a little on another leaf, all the time thinking very hard about the taste she would like it to have. She tried to remember what a leaf tasted like, and suddenly it became greener and juicier, and she chewed on it for a while. "Yes, you are right. It is starting to taste like a leaf now, you see!" The Kitchen Giraffe was delighted.

"We have all been summoned to this planet for a reason, I am sure. I would very much like to know for what I am appropriate."

"I am more worried about my properties," said the Kitchen Giraffe, still chewing on the imaginary leaf. "Why do you think I have these stripes? Do giraffes have stripes? I don't know, you see. But I have a nice hat."

"A hat! Ha! That's a funnel, Kitchen Giraffe. And I think it might even be the reason why you are called Kitchen Giraffe."

"What are you talking about, Wood Hound? What is a funnel anyway? It is my hat! And you, are you a Wood Hound because of your tail?"

The Famous Wood Hound tried to turn around and have a look at his tail which made him twirl a little, as every time he thought he had reached his tail, it switched to the other side.

The animals laughed.

"Yes, I think my tail is a fir tree, but I am the Famous Wood Hound because of my famous blueberry pies."

"Indeed I think we are here because of you. You and your famous blueberry pies," the Kitchen Giraffe ventured.

"Well, well, well. My blueberry pies certainly do allow travel across parallel worlds," the Famous Wood Hound admitted. "But the only one who knows how to do this is Tigah."

"Tigah! Where is he by the way?"

"He is on Earth now, I think, or in the Imagination, I am not sure. He said he had a mission - something about the Nuzzle with the Muzzle. I don't know exactly."

"The Nuzzle with the Muzzle, you see, that's what bears do. And I think we are here to learn how to do this."

"But Tigah said cats do that, and it is their invention, not the bears'," said the Famous Wood Hound.

"It might be another variation of the same thing, don't you think? Wheeeheeehee!" ventured the Appropriate Horse.

While the non-bears delved deeper and deeper into the discussion on the possible origins and variations of the Nuzzle with the Muzzle, Adelaide and Bearmouse had made their way to the Bear Park. Nanuk was still wandering about, hoping to see a bear appear, spontaneously.

"Nanuk!" Adelaide called. "What are you doing here?"

"Squeak!" Bearmouse added, just in case.

"Hello Adelaide! Hello Bearmouse! I am waiting for a bear, of course. What else would I be doing here?"

"Ah, very well. But tell us, have you seen any animals that were not bears, by any chance?"

Nanuk put his paw on his chin and said "Mmm, let me think. Yes, I think I saw animals! I am not sure what they were. You know my memory is fading quickly, but I remember someone saying 'you see' all the time, which was quite annoying."

"Nanuk, please try to focus. What animals did you see, and where did they go?" Adelaide asked, her voice trembling a little.

"I just know that they were not bears, and you said that bears appear spontaneously in the Bear Park, and that's why I am here. I want to see a bear appear out of the blue. A bear!" Nanuk became a little impatient, and nervous too. He had written down the information on a little note and shook it in front of Bearmouse's nose. He was after all on the planet of bears, and all he had seen in the Bear Park were animals that were not bears.

"All right, calm down, Nanuk. We need to find the new animals now!"

"They can't have gone far," Nanuk added. "And also, they were not bears," mumbling to himself as he walked away.

Adelaide took Bearmouse by the paw and dragged him a little further. She had spotted a strange looking tail disappear behind a bush. "Come along, I think I saw something interesting."

And they quickly found themselves facing the three strange-looking animals discussing the Nuzzle with the Muzzle.

"Wheeheehee! The Nuzzle with the Muzzle! What is that anyway?" the Appropriate Horse asked, in irritation and shaking his mane.

"It is our invention!" Adelaide said. "Teddy Bear and Faufur invented it in order to make children happy. And also, I teach a workshop that every bear must attend before he is sent to Earth."

"Oh, Adelaide! You found us!" cried the Kitchen Giraffe, lowering her head a little. She blushed. Turning toward the others, she said "She found us, you see!"

"Squeak! Yes, we need to discuss your presence among us. What are you doing here?" asked Bearmouse.

"Well, …we traveled through the Imagination, as all imaginary animals do, and suddenly we arrived on the planet of the bears. Isn't that strange?" asked the Kitchen Giraffe, without adding 'you see' this time.

"Very strange," agreed Adelaide. "You are definitely not bears. That is certain."

"Squeak! All imaginary animals travel through the Imagination? Why is that?"

"In order to become plush animals, you see. We have been called by wishes."

"But you don't have Wish Captors, I will have to attach one to each of you."

"But, will we become bears too?" asked the Wood Hound, suddenly worried about his Wood Pie Bakery.

"No, of course not. You will have Wish Captors customized with your own features." Adelaide had quickly adjusted to the situation, although she dreaded President Teddy Bear's reaction to this new development.

"Tell me more about Imagination, please," said Bearmouse.

"There is a certain number of properties, and when some of them fit particularly well together, they create an animal which evolves into an entity that comes into existence in the Imagination."

"That is fascinating. And how do the animals get their shape? You know that we bears get our shape from watching the bears on Earth."

"But you can become real. That is why you watch the bears on Earth. We are pure figments of Imagination right now. Maybe that is the reason why we are here?" The Wood Hound thought aloud.

"So, the planet of bears will become the planet of all animals?" Adelaide wondered. "Teddy Bear will be very upset."

"Teddy Bear will have to understand that bears are not the only animals in the universe that matter."

"But, the Nuzzle with the Muzzle! It is fundamental that plush animals know how to do that!" Adelaide added, starting to worry about her workshop.

"Of course, all plush animals will have to know how to do the Nuzzle with the Muzzle. But they don't need to be bears for that. Wheeheeehee!" said the Appropriate Horse shaking his very appropriate muzzle.

"So do you think you came here in order to become plush animals like us?" Bearmouse asked.

"Wheheehee! That could well be," the Appropriate Horse said.

"We would have to watch animals like us on Earth, then? The way you do?" The Wood Hound objected, wondering if such animals even existed.

"Well, maybe you don't need to watch animals on Earth if you have already been created by wishes. We watch the bears because we need to look like them. Children like to recognize the real bear quality in their plush animals. But maybe all this is not as essential as we thought."

Bearmouse looked at the new animals and decided that it was perhaps time that the planet opened up to new inhabitants.

"We have to talk to Teddy Bear. And we have to call in a meeting!"

"Bear up!" Everybody said, almost at the same time.

"Clong!"

Tigah had traveled through the Imagination again after stopping at Faunour's office and was now back in the Wood of the Same Name so that he could eat more blueberry pie for his travel to Alas-K. He was standing in front of the Woof Pie Bakery, and tried knocking. It was a little difficult with his soft paws. It sounded more like he was tapping the door gently.

"Famous Wood Hound? Ademar? Are you there?" Tigah called inside the house. Nobody answered.

Tigah noticed that the door was ajar and a piece of rope was tied to the handle. He slowly opened it a little wider and peeked inside.

The room was full of pies on displays of different sizes and the pies looked all very appetizing. In the middle of the room there was a counter.

"I need some blueberry pie because I need to travel to Alas-K, but the Famous Wood Hound must have left already. Mmm…," he said, more to himself. But then he heard a sound.

Tigah called out "Who is there?"

"Clong!"

"Sorry?"

"Clong." There was the sound again.

"Where is my Appropriate Horse?" someone said from behind the counter, followed by "Clong!"

"Your what?" Tigah asked.

"My Appropriate Horse! I have been looking for it for ages. For ages!"

Tigah jumped on the counter and looked down. There was a bear in armor. He was wearing a helmet that was far too big for his head, although his ears poked out from little holes provided for them. His visor kept shutting down, which produced the sound "Clong!"

"Who are you?" Tigah asked, and stretched out one paw.

"I am the Knight of the Round Ear. And I need my Appropriate Horse." The bear tried to get up, but his armor kept him from finding his balance and he flailed around helplessly on the floor.

"I see," Tigah said. "It looks like you could use some help."

"You think?" The Knight said impatiently. "I can't seem to get up," he added and tried to grab hold of something to help him get up, but his visor kept closing and he couldn't see anything. Then he fell down again.

"Wait, let me throw this rope to you." Tigah picked up the piece of rope from the door, and threw one end of it to the bear. "Try to hold on to that, I will pull you up."

After a lot of effort and concentration, Tigah and the Knight of the Round Ear managed to face one another.

"Hello. Thank you. Oh my, you are a cat," the Knight said with a sigh of relief, the moment he was standing upright again. In the split second his visor managed to stay open, he had caught a quick glimpse of Tigah.

"Yes, I am. I am Tigah, and you are a bear. Shouldn't you be on Alas-K, the planet of bears? What are you doing here?"

"Well, I don't know, really. I was looking for my Appropriate Horse, and then I fell into the Imagination. The Horse must have been here, too?"

"What is an Appropriate Horse, if you don't mind explaining?" Tigah tilted his head to one side.

"The Horse that I need. My Appropriate Horse. There is nothing to explain." The Knight stated stubbornly. And his visor closed again.

"All right. Do you know about the blueberry pies?"

"Oh, yes. They help you travel across parallel worlds. But sometimes you get lost, like me."

"You didn't eat them the right way, I suppose. I will show you. Do you want to go back to your planet?"

"Yes, of course. It will soon be time for the Bear Festival and I have to be there. I am responsible for the Nuzzle Competition."

"So, we will have to find the right way to eat the blueberry pie then. I have to go to Alas-K myself."

"But you are a cat! Cats are not allowed on the planet of the bears!"

"And why is that?" Tigah asked innocently.

"You know why. The Nuzzle with the Muzzle, cats think that it is their invention."

"But it is, and I need to tell the bears that!" Tigah insisted.

"No, you don't. The Nuzzle with the Muzzle is what bears do." The Knight of the Round Ear took up his sword and waved it around a little. Tigah dodged.

"You need my help to go back to your planet, so stop that," Tigah said and dodged again when the sword came dangerously close to his tail.

"What do you suggest then, cat?" The Knight stopped waving his sword but still had a little trouble with his balance, and his visor made the "Clong!" sound again the moment he stopped moving.

"What animals are allowed on the planet?"

"Bears mostly, but anyone I think, except cats and rabbits."

"Rabbits?"

"Yes, bunnies. They are the bears' primary rivals. Bears don't like them very much."

"I see."

"But tigers are allowed, I would say. Can you become a tiger?" The Knight suggested out of the blue.

"Well…I think so, after all, my name is Tigah. If there is a connection between coming into existence and properties, there certainly must be a connection between a name and existence."

"Then what should we do?"

"We can try using the pies."

Tigah looked around the room and the pies seemed to sparkle. Stars glowed around them and sometimes a ray of light came out of one pie, then jumped on to the next, leaving behind a stream of stars.

"We could follow the stars. The Wish Captors have stars on them, don't they?"

"I think they do, but how do you know that, cat?" The bear did not trust Tigah.

"Everybody knows that," Tigah said.

"No. Nobody knows that in fact. Only the bears who arrive on Alas-K and get a Wish Captor attached to their tummies by Adelaide know that!" "Clong!" The Knight suddenly realized that he had undoubtedly said too much and took up his sword again.

"All right, bear. Calm down. I know this from the teddy bear we have at home. He told me."

"How can he talk to you about those things? He is supposed to be numb and asleep and a puppet and not know anything about anything, much less talk to a cat about it!"

"Nelson can do anything."

"Ah, Nelson is your bear! Now I understand." The Knight became quite agitated and lost his balance again. He stumbled and fell on his back.

Tigah jumped on the bear's armored tummy and said "Bear, we can help each other, or stay in this Wood Pie Bakery forever! What do you say?" and Tigah put his nose close to the Knight's visor and purred.

"All right, all right. Just help me up." The bear tried to find back on his feet but not only did his armor keep him from moving and his visor kept shutting down, now Tigah had also put his paws on his chest and pushed him down.

"Your paws are very soft." The Knight of the Round Ear noted.

"Yes, I know."

Tigah grabbed the piece of rope again and jumped on the counter. The bear held on to it and was back on his paws in no time. Although Tigah had soft paws, he had a lot of strength.

"Thank you, Tigah. So, what do you suggest we do to make you a tiger?"

"I think we need a wish in order to do that. We were all created by wishes."

"But you are a cat, a real Earth cat. No wish created you!"

"How do you know that?" Tigah asked, turning to the Knight with a threatening purr.

"I...I don't. It seems to me that animals on Earth are created by something that is called biology. But of course, I am no expert."

"Sure, biology, and why would that not involve wishes, too?"

"Indeed, why not? But again: how do we make you a tiger?"

"Someone has to wish for a tiger. You know I could appear in Faunour's office just because he had programmed my key features into the Wish Captor Manipulator. So, if the tiger's properties came up somehow, I could jump in!"

"Interesting. And how do we trigger the wish for a tiger?"

What they didn't know was that their very conversation had already created the wish they needed.

Anton had crawled into bed that night, had taken Nelson, his favorite bear, in one arm and stretched out the other to find Tigah beside his bed, as he did every night. But Tigah was not there. Anton, alarmed, jumped out of bed again, with Nelson still tucked under his arm, and looked under the bed, inside the closet, behind the shoes, in the bathroom and even on the top shelf of his bookcase, a hiding place he knew Tigah particularly liked. But Tigah was nowhere to be found.

Anton didn't want to bother his dad, so he went back to bed and Nelson jumped on his chest.

After saying "Mmm Hmm" a few times, he had found the perfect spot to do the Nuzzle with the Muzzle, and Anton felt the bliss and the joy the Nuzzle created and knew that Tigah was all right, and he fell asleep quickly and soundly, and he dreamed of a bakery in the woods and blueberry pies. He dreamed that a tiger would allow him to travel to the planet of the bears, and he dreamed that Bearmouse liked tigers and wanted to meet one, more than anything.

Tigah suddenly felt the need to stretch and his paws seemed to be growing. When he looked at them he saw that they were indeed getting bigger and stronger, and he could even feel his claws grow as well.

"Bear! I think it is working. Quick, please get us some blueberry pie, and then we will travel to Alas-K. I will show you how."

In amazement, the Knight of the Round Ear watched Tigah transform into a tiger. Big Creamy would have been happy to witness such a puzzling event. He was, after all, the Secretary of Puzzlement. Tigah's body now grew bigger and his off-white stripes turned into black stripes, and his ginger fur became caramel brown.

"You are a tiger all right," he said, astonished.

"How did that work so quickly?"

"Wishes are wonderfully powerful things, Knight. Mrrreeow!" Tigah was now growling and his meowing started to sound a little more threatening. "I am a tiger now! A tiger!" Tigah announced triumphantly, and began to pounce around at random. "Mrrreeow!"

"You know what, Tigah," said the Knight of the Round Ear. "You have round ears now, too. Like us."

"Mreeow! Tigers are cats with round ears. That's why they are allowed on the planet Alas-K."

The Knight of the Round Ear took one blueberry pie in his paws. He tried not to crush it with his gauntlet and Tigah put his now big, strong paws under it to keep it from falling. "Clong!"

"Thanks, Knight. I think, we have to turn it a little, like this, and then cut a piece from the left corner like this, and then finally take a bite from the right side. Like that."

And Tigah demonstrated the right way to eat the blueberry pie in order to travel to the planet Alas-K. Tigah took a bite and gave the bear one, just before his helmet shut itself again.

"Hoimsli," the bear said.

"Hoimsli indeed," said Tigah and they shared an exceptional moment of superb taste when they both had their bite of blueberry pie.

"So, are you ready, Knight?" Tigah asked, when he saw that the stars had started forming around them.

"It is imperative we travel on the right stars. Do you notice how they twirl a little, and then light up? When they are aligned, they form a path and we can walk on them, like stardust, you see. We can travel along the pathway of stars all the way to Alas-K, if we get our first steps right. Ready?"

"Clong!" went the Knight's helmet. The bear licked his muzzle and swallowed the last piece of pie.

"Yes, Tigah, I'm ready. Wait, I need to open my visor." And the bear looked around and tried to put his paws on the right stars. Tigah had found the right star to start his journey, and then put one paw on an exceptionally bright star that turned red when he touched it. The next star lit up and Tigah put his paw on that star, and so on and so forth, until he had found the four correct stars that would guide him to the planet of the bears.

The Knight of the Round Ear had a little more trouble keeping his balance and at first tried to catch the stars instead of putting his paws on them.

The stars expanded a little and made more room for the bear's paws, and although he felt a little shaky and was scared to look down, he managed to find his star path as well.

His stars were silver, like his armor.

"Mreeow!" said Tigah. "Bear up! Let's go see the bears!"

And the Knight of the Round Ear had a split second to wonder how Tigah knew the secret motto of the MOLOB before a stream of stars swallowed them both up and led them through the Imagination, straight to the planet of the bears.

Or not exactly.

"I feel a little transparent"

Hazelnut had arrived early that morning. He had called the observation group for a meeting. Meanwhile, Little Creamy had more trouble with his huge screwdriver than usual and was a little late.

"Bears, I want you to concentrate very hard on your shape today," Hazelnut said. "We will watch the bears on Earth and I want you to try and notice the immediate effect that watching them has on you. If you have any questions, please let me know."

The bears did not ask any questions, but they mumbled to each other instead on the way to their posts.

"Hey, bear!"

"Yes, indeed, I am a bear. You are a bear, too."

"Yes, indeed, I am a bear."

"What about the shape?"

"Don't know. My shape is not very stable yet, can you tell? I feel a little transparent."

"Let me see your Wish Captor."

"Indeed, the stars on your Wish Captor do not seem very colored. They have not caught enough wishes for the shape yet."

"Do you think we have to watch the bears to get our shape?"

"Maybe so."

"Mm Hmm. Yes, I think so too," said the other bear.

And the two bears took their post at the telescopes and adjusted the eyepiece to their height. Lifting their arms and bending their muzzles, they started their observation session for the day.

"Oh, look at that one. What a beautiful, majestic bear!" The first bear said.

"Indeed, what a magnificent bear!"

And the moment they said that, a wave of trembling shook through them.

"Hey, look at my shape," the second bear said, shaking his head.

And indeed, the second bear had a better contour somehow, as if a line had been drawn around him. He seemed to stand out sharper from the background.

"You are much sharper now. You are starting to look more and more like a bear," the first bear said.

"Thank you, bear. The bears on Earth send contours to our shape."

The first bear looked through the eyepiece again and suddenly his body filled up with color little by little. He became a full and round brown bear. He shook himself a few times, put one paw on his muzzle, and stretched.

"You are a brown bear now. Like the one we just saw," the second bear said.

"Darn! Why do you keep doing that?" Little Creamy who had more trouble with his screwdriver than usual had finally arrived at the observation station. "Hello, bears! I am so sorry, my screwdriver is misbehaving today. I don't know what is the matter with him. How are you today? Did you get a better shape by watching the bears on Earth?"

The first bear and the second bear eagerly told Little Creamy that their shape had indeed improved in clarity and sharpness. Little Creamy was glad to hear that the bears had seen beautiful bears on Earth that had given them a better shape, and when they told him their story, the screwdriver almost jumped out of his paw. "I get it. It wants to tell me something."

The screwdriver had started walking on its own and was heading towards Adelaide's Nuzzle with the Muzzle Workshop. "I am sorry, bears. You will have to do the flipbooks with Hazelnut today. It seems I have some very important business to attend to." And Little Creamy started running after his screwdriver, while the bears protested a little and complained that the EMOT seemed to be more preoccupied with his screwdriver than with them.

"Who has touched the
Magic Potions?"

The Kitchen Giraffe looked around the Bear Park and noticed that what she had tried with the leaf seemed to work for everything else as well. When she looked at something, it suddenly had more color and more shape. When she turned her eyes away, things seemed to fall back into a grey, moving state. But she had to look away really fast and back again to notice this. She tried to move her head more quickly in order to see the moment when things faded into the grey state, but she could not move her head fast enough. Everything seemed perfectly shaped every time she looked at it. When she concentrated on something, it became focused, had color and shape and sense. Like the leaf she had for breakfast, other things seemed to become fuller and more defined when she concentrated very hard on them. She had tried it with grass, flowers, and even some patches of sky. It seemed as if she created things just by looking at them.

The Kitchen Giraffe walked a little further among the trees in the Bear Park. The trees looked perfectly normal, like trees on Earth. But inside the hollows of the tree trunks, the Kitchen Giraffe noticed peculiar looking bottles. She had heard about the existence of squirrel storage places in tree trunks, so she supposed those bottles had to be some kind of treasure and she tried to nibble on them, thinking they might contain some kind of tasty juice. She pushed one with the tip of her nose and the pink liquid inside shook a little. She pushed again, and the bottle fell to one side. It was closed, but the cork seemed loose so she gave it a little nudge, and it came off. She smelled the liquid and thought that it did not have much smell, as the things on Alas-K seemed to, usually, they were transparent and without contour until you imagined and wished for something and concentrated very hard on them.

"Kitchen Giraffe, what are you doing?" called Adelaide, interrupting her discovery. "We need to get to the workshop right away and find Wish Captors for you before Teddy Bear finds out that you are here!"

"Yes, Adelaide, just a second. I found something very interesting, you see."

"What did you find?" Adelaide took Bearmouse by the paw again, and the Appropriate Horse and the Famous Wood Hound followed closely.

"Woof!"

"Wheeeheeehee! What's going on? Kitchen Giraffe, what have you been doing?"

"Look at these bottles. Do you know what they are for?"

"The bottles! Bearmouse, the bottles!" Adelaide was extremely alarmed.

"Calm down, Adelaide! Calm down! As long as you don't think about what they are, you are fine."

The Kitchen Giraffe had spilled a little of the pink liquid on the tip of her nose.

"What did you do, Kitchen Giraffe?"

"Oh, was I not supposed to find these bottles? I thought they contained juice of some kind." She blushed a little bit and even forgot to add "you see" in her bewilderment. She turned away, and in the corner of her eye, she noticed that the tree was fading, but quickly, she turned back and there it was again, all brown and green. She shook her head and wondered if the others had noticed that too. But for now, they all seemed very excited about the discovery of the bottles in the tree hollow.

"These are the Magic Potions! The Magic Potions are hidden inside the tree hollows, and usually, nobody can see them, except Faufur and Teddy Bear because they are the only ones who know how to use them. But the new animals on the planet must have changed the outline of the world!"

"What are you saying? Adelaide, the outline of the world?"

"Yes, the Imagination, you know. We are kept in balance by the wishes and how they arrive on the planet. The Wish Captors, and the stars…"

"You are babbling, Adelaide. Why don't you sit down and relax," Bearmouse said and asked the new imaginary animals to wish for a bunch of chairs and some lemonade. Actual lemonade, and not some Magic Potion disguised as lemonade like the one the Kitchen Giraffe had found.

And the Wood Hound, the Appropriate Horse, the Kitchen Giraffe and Bearmouse concentrated very, very hard on the wish for chairs and a table. They appeared after a few moments, although their colors did not match, neither did their styles. As the Kitchen Giraffe had wished for bar stools, they all had one leg higher than the others, and the animals had to push the chairs' legs into the ground a little in order to be able to sit down on them.

"I am sorry," said the Kitchen Giraffe. Everybody looked at her, knowing exactly that it was her wish that had created the confusion. "What? They go well in a stylish kitchen, you see," she batted her eyelashes and looked down.

Adelaide sat on an uneven chair and sighed. "What shall we do? Teddy Bear must be aware of the non-bears. And what will he do? Will he send us all to Earth now? And what about the Nuzzle with the Muzzle?"

"Squeak!" Bearmouse said, impatiently. "Please calm down, Adelaide. We will find a solution."

"Wheeeheeehee! Indeed. I for example can do the Nuzzle with the Muzzle very well." And he rubbed his nose on Adelaide's cheek a few times, until she smiled again. She giggled and said "It's alright now, Appropriate Horse, thank you."

"Wheeeheehee! My pleasure."

"Hey! Stop that now, please!" Little Creamy was still running after his screwdriver that seemed to have lost all control and was sprinting through the Bear Park. Little Creamy begged the screwdriver to stop, as he was out of breath and panting. Fortunately, the screwdriver had at last found what he had been looking for and came to an abrupt halt.

"Phhhh! Thank you. Hello, all!" said Creamy before he sank down on the ground and laid flat on his back with exhaustion.

The screwdriver stopped in front of Adelaide and fell straight into her paw. "Hello, screwdriver," Adelaide said, not knowing what else to say to a screwdriver falling into her paw.

"Squeak!" said Bearmouse. "I think we need to get back to the workshop right away. The screwdriver must have a message for us." Everybody took a last sip from the lemonade and got up.

"Creamy, there is some lemonade for you," said Bearmouse before they left. Little Creamy was slowly recovering from his exhausting trip chasing after his screwdriver, and he was now lying on his back, panting. He looked up and saw the others had left him behind, then sank back down again. When he lifted himself up to see where the others had gone off to, he saw a few glasses of lemonade on the table and finished them up one after the other.

"Hoimsli!" He said and started heading toward the Bear Workshop as well. He was curious to know what the screwdriver had to tell them that was so important it could not wait. When Creamy left, the table, the chairs and the glasses of lemonade disappeared, as no one wished for them anymore.

"Zebras have stripes, but giraffes don't!"

Adelaide was still holding on to the screwdriver when they arrived at the Bear Workshop. Now that it had found her, it seemed to be perfectly calm. She opened the door. Inside the office, the screens were lit and all the symbols were blinking in great confusion. "Oh, what has happened to the screens?"

Adelaide threw her arms up in the air, her eyebrows knit up in a worried frown.

"Adelaide!"

When she heard that voice, she recoiled with fear, and motioned the others to hide.

"Teddy Bear! President! What brings you to my workshop?" Adelaide straightened her body and tried to appear calm.

Teddy Bear stepped out from behind the screens, glaring angrily.

"What is going on here?"

Teddy Bear was an old teddy bear, his fur was not as soft and cuddly anymore as it had once been. There were a few rough, worn out patches on his back and paws.

"The Wish Captors seem to catch properties that have nothing to do with bears! Stripes! Pointy ears! Long bushy tails! I demand an explanation!" Teddy Bear was very angry, and his big head seemed even bigger when he tried to tower over Adelaide, although they were about the same height.

"Oh, well, dear President, I think you know why this is happening. Or don't you?" Adelaide said, with confidence. She was not used to letting herself be intimidated, not even by the President himself.

"Are you referring to that renegade Faunour whom I have sent to Earth in order to keep our planet free from his disturbing ideas?"

"Well, I would not call him a renegade, President. After all, he is in charge of shipping our fellow bears to the children on Earth so that the bears can do the Nuzzle with the Muzzle."

"He has always wanted to make this planet a planet for everyone. But this is our planet, the planet of the bears. It was created as a refuge for the bears in distress and a place where bears could come into existence, nothing else."

"But President, why is opening the planet to other animals such a terrible idea after all?"

Adelaide asked, waving her arms in order to keep the Kitchen Giraffe, the Famous Wood Hound and the Appropriate Horse well hidden behind the door.

"Wheeheehee!" he said, softly.

"Hush, we have to hide, you see," said the Kitchen Giraffe.

"Woof!" barked the Wood Hound with a very soft voice.

The three of them huddled up closer together.

"What are you doing there, Adelaide?" asked Teddy Bear.

"Nothing," she said, trying to stay calm. "I have to arrange some things here, behind the door, you see."

"Opening the planet to other animals jeopardizes the importance of the bear in the minds of the children." Teddy

Bear explained. "They will not think anymore that teddy bears are the best plush animals, they will just consider them plush animals among others if there are other animals to choose from. Just think what happened with the bunnies!" Teddy Bear shivered.

"The bunnies, yes. We couldn't do anything about that, couldn't we? And now many children prefer to hold on to the long ears of the bunny instead of doing the Nuzzle with the Muzzle with a bear. Just think, if we opened the planet to other animals that will also do the Nuzzle with the Muzzle, maybe we could beat the bunnies again, President, don't you think?"

"Mhhh. Beat the bunnies? But how? By letting other animals do the Nuzzle with the Muzzle? But it is our thing. Our trademark, so to speak."

"But isn't it more the Nuzzle with the Muzzle that makes the bear so special? Opening up the training to many animals would make our trademark more widespread and well known and this could only be beneficial for us." Adelaide added, thinking about the possible future growth of her Nuzzle Training Workshop.

At that moment, the screens lit up again and a stream of stars poured out of each one of them. "Step back, pleaaaase!" Someone said, and Bearmouse grabbed Adelaide's paw at the last second.

Teddy Bear jumped back, when suddenly Tigah walked straight into the Bear Workshop on the path of red stars that had started in the Famous Wood Bakery.

"Hello there! I am Tigah! A cat...no... I mean...I am a tiger! Mrreoww! Yes, a tiger!" Tigah said when he landed in the workshop, and the stream of stars cooled down. He shook himself and arched his back.

"Wow!" said Bearmouse, suddenly letting go of Adelaide's paw. "Look at that! Magnificent!"

Adelaide turned to Bearmouse, and saw his face light up with amazement.

"Hello, Tigah," Adelaide said. "Good job in finding the right stars!"

"Thank you! I have brought someone with me! Mrreow!" Tigah stepped down from the pathway of stars and looked around the workshop. "Or haven't I? Where is he? Hello??? Knight of the Round Ear, where are you?"

"Wheeeheehee! A knight. Very interesting." The Appropriate Horse said from behind the door.

"Who are you?" asked Tigah, stretching out his left front paw, now strong and clawed.

"I am the Appropriate Horse! Wheeeheeheee," he said, and he shook his mane.

"Oh, that is excellent! The Knight will be so happy to see you! But where is he?" Tigah looked again, up and down, left and right. The Horse moved his head along with Tigah. The Knight of the Round Ear was nowhere to be seen.

"Did you lose someone, cat?" Teddy Bear suddenly stepped forward from behind the screens.

"But what are you talking about, I am not a cat. I am a tiger! Mrrreooooow!" Tigah roared.

"You can't fool me, cat. I can tell by your eyes that you are not really a tiger."

"I am just as much a tiger as you are a bear," Tigah said.

"A cat, a horse! Who else on the bear planet is not a bear?" Teddy Bear asked threateningly.

"Woooof! I am the Famous Wood Hound."

"Hello, Mister President, I am the Kitchen Giraffe. But this is not in any way meant to inconvenience you, you see." She tried to be very polite in order not to annoy him with her presence.

The Appropriate Horse, the Kitchen Giraffe and the Famous Wood Hound now stepped out from behind the door.

Teddy Bear looked at the Kitchen Giraffe in amazement.

"What happened to *you*? Giraffes don't have stripes," Teddy Bear snapped.

This sudden harshness was too much for her and she ran out of the workshop, sobbing.

"Kitchen Giraffe, wait!"

The Appropriate Horse and the Famous Wood Hound immediately ran after her.

"Now, look what you've done," Adelaide said to Teddy Bear who turned away, shamefaced.

"Hey, wait for me!" said Little Creamy who had finally arrived at the Bear Workshop.

"Wishes fly through the Imagination!"

"This is quite unpleasant, you see!"

The Kitchen Giraffe talked to herself as she ran and began crying. As she cried, she lost more and more touch with the ground, and the faster she ran the more the world became blurred, and she couldn't distinguish between things anymore. Eventually, she lost the desire to add "you see" to her thoughts, and her blue funnel hat flew off her head.

Suddenly, she seemed to slip off the planet of the bears into the Imagination. "Ohhh!" she cried, and her funnel shaped hat fell off when she was absorbed by the other dimension. Somehow, her distress had caused the Automatic Negation to activate, and because she had not yet received her Wish Captor, her existence in the world was not stable enough. Also, her sensitivity made her most vulnerable to sudden changes. When she stopped feeling loved, she was in danger of slipping back into possibility, and so she did.

Stars of all colors were shooting by her in all directions, and she could hear the whisper of the wishes as they passed her by. "I want a bear right now!" That wish was too vague and faded away, floated and twirled, until another one whispered: "I want my bear to have rounded ears." That one was precise enough and quickly left the Imagination and traveled to a Wish Captor on a bear on the planet Alas-K. "Oh!" The Kitchen Giraffe cried again, and tried batting her eyelashes, which was difficult with all the wishes twirling around her.

"That's very exciting, you see," she said to herself, and dazzled by all the colors and the lights, she had almost forgotten how Teddy Bear's insult had robbed her of her stability.

When she had last traveled through the Imagination, she had not been aware of the in-between state where the wishes actually flew around. She then must have been the object of a very precise wish at a very special moment in time. She had not known then that even when you were once wished for very dearly, you could be pushed into non-existence by one careless remark. She looked around and batted her eyelashes.

"I want a giraffe with stripes."

She heard that, and she giggled when the wish started shooting past her.

"What, a giraffe with stripes? That is utterly ridiculous. Zebras have stripes, not giraffes. We have been to the zoo and I have shown you the zebras, you silly child. Can't you listen and look? Stop dreaming and confusing everything!"

The Kitchen Giraffe was now also aware of the opposite wish that followed closely behind the desire to create a giraffe with stripes. She tried to look down on her coat, and saw threatening brown patches appear on her beautiful black and white stripes. "Oh no! What is happening to me? Help!" It seemed that she could not only lose her funnel hat, but her stripes as well.

Quickly, another wish followed that was focused on the giraffe with zebra-stripes, and she was partly restored. But then again, someone tried to teach a child that giraffes had brown patches, and that zebras had stripes.

The wish for the Kitchen Giraffe had paused nearby and started circling her. She did not have her Wish Captor and she generally did not feel very sure of her own existence, so the wish did not have a precise place to go. Still, it seemed to know that it had found the right place, and it stayed close to her.

"Hello, wish!" she said "I don't have my Wish Captor yet, you see. Adelaide got distracted, and then, Teddy Bear insulted my stripes. That was just more than I could bear, you see." The Kitchen Giraffe tried to explain. The wish swirled once around her, then remained close to her head. Other wishes started to gather around her. Usually, fully formed creatures only passed through Imagination without being aware of the wishes. It was an exceptional opportunity for wishes to see a creature, as they usually vanished when they reached a Wish Captor. So they stayed around the Kitchen Giraffe. The wishes said "Stripes!" "Long muzzle!" and one, lagging behind, said "Blue funnel hat!"

"Yes, my hat! Where is it?" The Kitchen Giraffe patted her head and noticed that her hat was gone. More and more wishes had found their way to the Kitchen Giraffe's head and slowly the outline of a blue funnel started to show on her head. She smiled and batted her eyelashes, and little by little her stripes were restored, although some wishes asked for a real giraffe and stopped by her for a moment, but then quickly moved further away.

"Wooof! Where is she?" The Wood Hound tried to find the trace of her smell. But on Alas-K, things did not really have a proper smell, so even for the Famous Wood Hound with his otherworldly sense of smell, it was difficult to find the trail of the Kitchen Giraffe. He sniffed alongside the Bear Workshop and went around in circles without even noticing. After a few times, he felt a little dizzy and said "Woof!" facing the Appropriate Horse again.

"Wheeeheehee! Kitchen Giraffe! Kitchen Giraffe!" called the Appropriate Horse. And then he saw her funnel hat lying on the ground. Just at the same time the Wood Hound stopped in front of it.

"Her hat!" When the Appropriate Horse picked it up, it seemed to be sparkling with stars.

"Wheeeheeehee! I know where she went! Look at the stars. She must have fallen into the Imagination. Oh dear, poor Kitchen Giraffe! She got so upset when Teddy Bear questioned her properties. Oh, I wish she wasn't that sensitive."

The Appropriate Horse and the Famous Wood Hound were at a loss to know what to do, when suddenly they heard a very loud crash.

The screwdriver had finally reached his destination and started to turn a screw on one of the screens.

When he had unloosened all the screws, the first screen fell off and revealed another one of a different texture. The screwdriver twirled a little and then fell down, with exhaustion.

"What was that?" Adelaide asked, turning her head towards Bearmouse who was about to go into a very prolonged "Squeaaak!"

"Another screen, another reality. Hey, I think I saw a …bunny ear."

"Bunny ear? You mean …?" Adelaide said.

Bunny Planet

The Knight of the Round Ear had found one, two, three silver stars to guide him back to the planet Alas-K where he belonged, the planet of the bears. But one star did not quite fit, and that one reluctant star did not know the way to Alas-K. That star was a bunny star. Therefore, instead of safely arriving on the planet of the bears, the Knight of the Round Ear found himself crashing down on the planet of the rabbits, the planet Alas-L.

Yes, the bunnies had their own planet, too. But there, it was not about the Nuzzle with the Muzzle, the rabbits were not even aware of its existence. The planet of the bunnies was a happy and mostly very cute place. As everyone on the planet hopped around constantly, stopping only to nibble on something before they continued hopping along, there was hardly any time to rest, and when no one was around to see the bunnies, they were all curled up in dens, sitting close to one another and nibbling away.

Since Earth boys and girls had discovered how cute bunnies were and how much it made them forget their worries when they looked at them, the bunnies had begun to disappear from their planet and arrive on Earth as plush rabbits, just like their cousins, the bears.

But for the bunnies, there was no moody rocket, no Robotbear, no telescopes, and no debate about the image or the properties. The rabbits simply slipped into Imagination and got their plush bunny shape there and when they had gathered enough wishes, they slipped right out on planet Earth. The system was not perfect, as for now, they arrived on Earth in parks, alleys, or even on beaches, totally at random, depending on where the last decisive wish came from. So, most of the time, a child marveled over a plush bunny and said to his mother "Look, Mom! Just the bunny I wished for!"

When the Knight of the Round Ear suddenly landed on the bunny planet, he could not see anything at first, of course, because of his visor. "Clong!"

"Hey, you!" He heard someone say. And it sounded like someone sniffed up his armored leg.

"What's that? Mm? What do you think?" "Well, I don't know, seems awfully big for a bunny. And shiny too!" Someone knocked on his armor.

The Knight of the Round Ear slowly raised his visor and opened it as carefully as he could and looked down. Two very small and bizarrely shaped creatures seemed to be circling around him.

"Hello, what are you?"

"What do you mean? What? We are rabbits, or bunnies as we are sometimes called. Especially, when we become plush animals."

"Plush animals? You become plush animals, too?"

"Of course, children find us in parks and take us home."

"Interesting system."

"Why is it interesting? What are you?"

"What? ...Well, I am a bear, you see. My name is Knight of the Round Ear."

The little bunnies started giggling as they noticed his protruding rounded ears. "Round ears indeed!"

"To you, it must seem funny, your ears are so long, and very far from round."

The bunnies jumped around a little and hopped away without even saying goodbye. The conversation they had just had with the bear was one of the longest a rabbit had ever had. They usually run away immediately when someone as much as looks at them.

The Knight of the Round Ear tried to enjoy the few moments his visor did not close and looked around. A giant screen stood in the middle of the landscape.

"Hey, Knight of the Round Ear, can you see me?" Adelaide called from the screen.

"Adelaide! What is going on here?" he asked and came closer to the screen.

"It seems you are on the bunny planet!"

"Yes, I have noticed that. But why can you see me?"

"Well, the screwdriver opened another screen window."

"What an amazing screwdriver!"

"He seems to connect worlds."

"Like the blueberry pies?"

"Maybe. So, what is it like on the bunny planet?"

"I don't know, they just hop around and nibble, even if there is nothing to nibble on."

"I see. You know that there is someone here you've been looking for."

"Really? Do you mean it has happened at last? Oh, how wonderful!" And the visor closed again, the Knight of the Round Ear had moved a little too abruptly.

"Yes, you will be happy to hear that the Appropriate Horse has finally made it to the planet of the bears. But for now, there is something more pressing that I need to tell you. We have lost the Kitchen Giraffe somewhere in the Imagination. You have to save her!"

"The Kitchen Giraffe? Who is that?"

"She has stripes, black and white stripes, like a zebra. And she wears a hat, a funnel hat."

"A funny hat?"

"A funnel hat."

"What's a funnel hat?"

"A hat that is a funnel, Knight of the Round Ear. Don't you know what a funnel is?"

"I …I…maybe I don't."

"Wait! Adelaide! Wait!" The Famous Wood Hound called out to her. "She has lost her hat! I found it. I don't know if she can get a new one in the Imagination." And the Famous Wood Hound entered the Bear Workshop carrying the funnel hat in his mouth.

Adelaide pointed at the funnel, and the Knight of the Round Ear nodded.

"Alright. I will see what I can do. But how do I leave this nibbling planet?"

"Well, you know what to do," Tigah said. "Reach into your left pocket, take the piece of pie out and take a bite from the right side."

Tigah had put a piece of blueberry pie in the armor pocket of the bear as he had a hunch that something might go a bit wrong on the way. Also, it was always a good idea to carry a piece of blueberry pie with you on a journey. You might get hungry.

"Oh, Tigah, you made it to Alas-K! Thanks a lot for planning ahead and anticipating my clumsiness."

The Knight of the Round Ear was a little offended that even Tigah had not trusted him to arrive immediately on Alas-K. He was a cat after all.

"Please, Knight. Just eat the pie and put your paws on the right stars. But on the way, stop in the Imagination and look for the Kitchen Giraffe! Good luck!"

The Knight of the Round Ear did as he was told and soon after having a bite of the Famous blueberry pie and turning it the right way, the stars lit up again and while he was still enjoying the taste extremely Hoimsli of the pie, he was already on his way. A few rabbits hopped around, but did not pay much attention to the big bear in armor that had spent such little time on their planet.

"Did you see? That was a bear? Amazing, right?"

"A bear? Oh! They also go to Earth and become plush animals, I think. Yes, but there are many more of us now."

"Good, good."

And they were on their way.

"My funnel hat!"

The Knight of the Round Ear took great care this time not to miss the fourth star that led to Alas-K. He also paid attention to his visor, as he needed to look out for the Kitchen Giraffe. The visor stayed open this time and the moment he stepped into the Imagination, he stopped the stars and looked around. Wishes were swirling and turning. When they noticed the Knight of the Round Ear, they stopped a little before they moved on. The Knight was a fully formed wish, he was very certain of where he wanted to go, and he knew that he needed his Appropriate Horse. Sometimes, he was a little clumsy and became a little distracted, but in general, his appearance was fully formed and his character was so strong that traveling through Imagination should not affect his stability. He would not go back to being a possibility. Not like the Kitchen Giraffe.

The Knight of the Round Ear did not know exactly how to find her, so he started asking the wishes.

"Hey! Do you know where I can find the Kitchen Giraffe?"

The wish that was closest to him needed to go to Alas-K quickly as he was meant for a brown bear so he brushed by him, and was gone. Wishes were very bright but they did not know how to respond to questions. Their information was visible and the Knight started to understand how to read the wishes by looking through them. He noticed that many wishes were about bears and many wishes were about rabbits but when he concentrated very hard he could see that some wishes were aimed at other animals and other shapes. He tried to concentrate on colors too, as he had noticed that the Kitchen Giraffe's hat, her funnel hat, was indigo blue.

The Knight moved around in the Imagination and, by looking through the wishes and listening to them, he understood some of the things that human children wanted most. When most of the wishes were about bears, he understood that children were sad and needed to be comforted, that they wished for a soft and pointy muzzle and round ears and the perfect bear shape so that they could hug a bear and not feel the disappointment, at least for a moment. The Knight shook off the feeling of sadness that traveled along with those wishes and then he continued to look around in the clouds of fog formed by the cluttered wishes. He tried to move slowly to keep his visor open.

"An Appropriate Horse!"

He suddenly heard a wish passing by closely and stopping for a moment. It was one of his wishes. The Appropriate Horse wish had no particular quality as the Knight had never explained to anyone why he needed an Appropriate Horse. The Knight of the Round Ear and his Appropriate Horse - the perfect picture. His wish had created a random horse, an expression of pure horse-ness so to speak. Only when the horse had met the giraffe and the dog on the way and they had formed a group, had he developed distinct character traits of his own. The horse now had a special fondness for bears, and as he was appropriate he assumed that he would be able to do the Nuzzle with the Muzzle in a very accomplished manner. A knight needed a horse. Everybody knew that. The Knight of the Round Ear was convinced that he must have had the perfect horse long ago but lost it, because of his clumsiness. He had decided that his ill-fitting armor was perfect for him, so that no one could hurt him or get to him, and one day, he would certainly get his Appropriate Horse back. That was all he cared about.

"It's not a *funny* hat, you see. It is a *funnel* hat!"

The Kitchen Giraffe tried to explain to the wishes for a "funny hat" that they were not in the right place. Sometimes wishes could get distracted by bad pronunciation.

"My hat is not funny. It is a beautiful *funnel* hat, you see," she repeated with determination, carefully enunciating the word "funnel."

It was then that the Knight of the Round Ear spotted the Kitchen Giraffe in the middle of a swirl of wishes, where nothing was defined, no shapes or colors existed when your mind was closed to them. Nothing was perceptible unless you let go of all previous knowledge and conviction. There he saw this creature who was left abandoned to the nothingness of indistinct wishes, but still so concerned about her hat that she had finally forgotten her despair, defending the color and the shape and even the purpose of a hat that was shaped like a funnel.

"It is a very important tool! To put liquid in a bottle, you see. And if I don't wear my hat, I am just a regular striped giraffe without any connection to a kitchen. Although, my name itself applies to a kitchen tool, a mixer, or a stick blender as it is sometimes called, you see."

In order to defend herself and to avoid the possibility state that would send her into despair, she had to stand up for herself even though she was not sure of what she was exactly. She was quite surprised at the things that came to mind when looking for a description of the wishes she needed in order to stay alive.

"Hey! You must be the Kitchen Giraffe!"

The Knight of the Round Ear had been watching her for a while and began to feel something like butterflies in his stomach. As he had never experienced this kind of feeling before, he had no idea what that meant.

"Oh! Excuse me, wishes. I think somebody is calling me, you see."

And she turned her head first to one direction and then to another, and then she tried to make a circle with her head, as there was no right way up in the Imagination. The Imagination did not have directions, so it seemed to her that by turning her head, different layers might be uncovered in this undefined world.

"Kitchen Giraffe!"

The Knight called again, and he noticed that his voice was fading a little when he called her. He cleared his throat and tried again.

"Kitchen Giraffe!"

"Yes, what is it? Who is calling me?"

"Over here! It's me! The Knight of the Round Ear!"

"Oh, are you a bear?" The Kitchen Giraffe asked with distinct disapproval.

"Yes, I am."

"Bears don't like me. And I am not so sure that I like them very much either, you see."

"But I am here to take you back to Alas-K."

"The planet of bears, where all they do is insult me? No, thank you. I prefer to stay a possibility, maybe something better will become of me here."

She raised her muzzle and turned her long neck away from the bear.

"Come on," he said, and even stretched out his arms to her.

"No, thank you. I'd rather stay here." And in the corner of her eye, a little tear formed.

"Come on, Kitchen Giraffe! I will set up the Nuzzle Competition and it is going to be great fun, you will see."

Quite used to making his point, the Knight of the Round Ear tried to convince the Kitchen Giraffe to go back to Alas-K by being firm, decisive and charming all at once.

"The Nuzzle Competition?"

"Yes, the game that allows us to determine the winners of the month. The bears who will travel to Earth as teddy bears, the ones with the best shape and the best ability to do the Nuzzle with the Muzzle."

"Do you participate in that?" The Kitchen Giraffe asked the Knight of the Round Ear.

"No, I only put everything in place and I coach the bears beforehand, with Adelaide's help."

"You coach them? How can you do that, when you don't do the Nuzzle with the Muzzle yourself?"

The Knight of the Round Ear looked at the Kitchen Giraffe, and found that she had quite an annoying way to ask questions.

"I just tell them what to do, that's my job. All pretty basic, you know. I really should be going back there to do it now. So, if you don't mind, could we speed this along?"

"Why don't we stay here for a while, in the possibilities."

"You have to do things, know what is right."

"I don't know what is right, you see."

"Of course you do."

The Knight of the Round Ear had not anticipated any resistance from her. He had started on his search, convinced that the Kitchen Giraffe was lost in the Imagination and wanted to go home. He had a clear and simple mission that Adelaide had given him. But suddenly, everything seemed much more complicated. He looked at the Giraffe and found her suddenly so exquisite that he could not believe his own reaction. "Clong! Clong!" his visor went, even twice, from the excitement.

The Kitchen Giraffe was in the middle of defending her very special identity in a flow of conflicting wishes that rushed by her and swirled and sometimes covered her completely.

"My blue funnel hat is essential to my head, and so are my stripes!"

And every time she asserted that, the Knight of the Round Ear witnessed a stronger coloration in her stripes. The hat itself, however, needed to be recreated as there was nothing but a flicker on her head in the shape of a blue funnel.

"I need my hat, you see! I am the Kitchen Giraffe!"

Looking at her, the Knight of the Round Ear began to realize that it might help her endeavor if he also believed in her.

"This is the Kitchen Giraffe, you see. She has black and white stripes and a blue funnel hat!"

He said to the wishes. With his help, the hat slowly settled into a stable enough shape to sit firmly on her head, between her ears.

She looked up, and when she felt that her hat had stabilized, she looked upon the bear in armor in a very different way.

"Thank you, Knight! You gave me back my hat!"

"Oh!" "Clong!" "No problem, Kitchen Giraffe. I mean, you need your hat if you want to make it in the world, right?" He mumbled.

"Oh, this is so very lovely of you!" And she batted her eyelashes at him.

His blushing went unnoticed, as he was well hidden inside his armor. "No need to thank me, really. Clong!"

"Of course, I need to thank you! You gave me back my existence!"

"Well, you seemed so ambivalent in your state."

"Ambivalent? Well, this is how we are supposed to be here, in the realm of possibilities. This is what Imagination is really all about, you see."

"Ah, is it really? I thought it was the place where we have to go through very quickly in order to reach action."

"Yes, that might be true, too. But sometimes we need to dwell on things for a bit. Only when you look at things from different perspectives you will understand them well, and act right, you see."

"No, just trust your intuition and act. When the moment passes, you move on to something else."

"Come on, Knight! You saved my life! Why can't you accept that things are not that simple?"

"I did what I had to do. That's just the way it is. Can we go home now? I don't want to talk about it."

"Sure, we can go home. But maybe you would like to reconsider something first?"

"What?"

"Don't you want a visor that allows you to see the world?"

"Mrr," the Knight said in a very bearish manner. It was the first time that someone had questioned the fact that his visor closed up every time he moved. The Kitchen Giraffe was the first creature to address his visor problem, but she thought it wise not to suggest ridding himself of the armor once and for all. Fixing the visor would already be a vast improvement, but for the Knight, it was already too much.

"I like it that way. I have had this visor for a long time, and it suits me perfectly and this is the way I want to live." The Knight said in his stubborn, matter-of-factly stern voice.

"But, Knight, it makes this obnoxious "Clong!" sound every time you move and when you fall you can barely manage to get up again!"

"How do you know that? I don't fall."

"Well, things don't stay secret in the Imagination. Tigah helped you up numerous times when you met in the Famous Wood Hound's Bakery. I suppose I would call that falling down, you see."

The Knight looked at her, and waited. He wanted to say "Come on", but she did not realize what she had just said.

And then there was this moment. When she pointed out this weakness, the Knight of the Round Ear remembered why he was wearing his armor after all, and a sudden flash of memory came back to him. There used to be a time, long before the armor, when he was vulnerable and innocent too, but that was a very long time ago.

"I have given you your hat back. That's all I can do for you."

The Knight turned away, breathing heavily. The Kitchen Giraffe tapped on his shoulder with her front hoof.

"Hey, don't be mad," she felt in her knees that she had said something wrong.

"I am not mad," he said, stubbornly. "But really, can we go now?"

"Everything happens so fast. It is difficult to adjust to the present."

"You are not even trying."

"I am. Don't be mean!" Now the Kitchen Giraffe turned away from the bear. But he did not persist.

"What is happening?" She asked herself.

"The bears are waiting for us. What are you doing?"

"I don't know. I lost something."

"Things are here and gone. Deal with it. If you don't act fast, they slip away, and they don't come back again."

"How can you say that?"

"That's just the way it is. On our planet, there is no memory, so no dwelling on events can happen. Can we please go now?"

"All right. Let's go back to the planet of the bears." The Kitchen Giraffe caved, and she would have had to regret this for a very, very long time had she not at the same time agreed to live on a planet of forgetfulness. "Did you bring enough blueberry pie for both of us?" She asked, wiping a tear from the corner of her eye.

"Let's see," said the Knight and reached into the pockets of his armor. "Of course, here you go."

And he handed the Kitchen Giraffe just the right amount of blueberry pie she needed to return to Alas-K safely. He wanted to make sure they would not land on another planet like the bunny planet.

"Hoimsli!" the Kitchen Giraffe said. "Thanks. I appreciate it!"

And when they both ate the blueberry pie, the stars lit up and showed the way.

The Kitchen Giraffe offered her hoof and the Knight took it, although he was still annoyed with her, however, he found her hard to resist. By holding on to one another, their balance was restored. The stars lined up perfectly.

"We have Wish Captors now!"

After traveling through the Imagination once more, the Kitchen Giraffe and the Knight of the Round Ear arrived safely at the Bear Workshop, where Adelaide, Bearmouse, Little Creamy, the Famous Wood Hound and the Appropriate Horse had been waiting for them in anxious anticipation.

"Woof! Finally!" said the Famous Wood Hound.

"Wheeheehee!" said the Appropriate Horse. "The Knight of the Round Ear!"

"Hello, Appropriate Horse! Good that you are here," the Knight said, removing the remaining stardust from his armor. "Let's catch up later, I have to go to work now. I am already late. Adelaide, the Nuzzle Competition starts in two days."

Adelaide looked at them in great confusion. "What happened in the Imagination?" She wanted to know.

"Squeak!" said Bearmouse, looking around. Tigah was licking his paws. He had found some left over crumbs of blueberry pie.

The Appropriate Horse was surprised at such a cool welcome coming from the Knight of the Round Ear, but he was very happy to see the Kitchen Giraffe again and quickly forgot about it. "You have your funnel hat back!" said the Appropriate Horse. "I tried to hold on to it for you, but it disappeared."

"Thank you, but everything is fine, you see. I have my hat back now." The Kitchen Giraffe started to feel the effects of memory loss that happened when one arrived on Alas-K. She knew that her stability was restored, but she also felt that something was not quite right.

"Clong!" went the visor of the Knight of the Round Ear. "Adelaide, come with me, we need to pick up Hazelnut."

"Wait, I need to install the Wish Captors on the new animals first. We don't want them to slip into Imagination again, don't we?"

And Adelaide busied herself choosing the right Wish Captor for the Kitchen Giraffe first, as the giraffe seemed to be in danger of slipping into possibilities again.

"So, let's see. Black and white stripes, blue funnel hat…" And she quickly found the right Wish Captor and set it up on the Kitchen Giraffe's tummy.

"Oh well, thank you Adelaide! That is very kind of you, you see," the Kitchen Giraffe said, and with her new Wish Captor her shape immediately stabilized.

"Woof!" Can I get mine too?"

And Adelaide looked for the Famous Wood Hound's Wish Captor among the pile. Most of them were still only set up for bear properties, but she managed to find the one that said "fir-tree tail" and understood that this one was meant for the Famous Wood Hound.

"I need to go back to my bakery. I will not stay here forever, you know."

„All new animas should wear a Wish Captor, just in case they develop wishes!"

"But are you sure that I won't become a bear?" The Wood Hound asked, worried that he might not be able to take care of his bakery, being a bear.

"No, of course not. You have your own properties: pointy nose, fir-tree tail, long body and short legs."

"Woof! Perfect. Thank you, Adelaide!"

Teddy Bear was pacing impatiently around the Workshop. "Mrrr," he said from time to time.

"Other animals! Ha! Mrrr!"

"Weeheheee! What about me?" said the Appropriate Horse.

"Well, you are special. There are some very precise wishes that concern you. Wait." And Adelaide found the Wish Captor that had already a few different shapes that had put on more color than the others. "You were created by a bear."

"Weeheeehee!" said the Horse.

"Yes, you are my Appropriate Horse!" said the Knight of the Round Ear, interrupting his preparation for the Nuzzle Competition for a second, but then continued his work right away.

"The Wish Captor for the Appropriate Horse has three half-moon shapes. They are all full of color and I don't think it will catch more wishes. I have never seen that before," Adelaide said while she attached the Wish Captor to the Appropriate Horse.

"What? A bear who wishes for a horse? What is going on here?" Teddy Bear muttered, and paced some more.

"Squeak! Calm down, President! Don't worry, we need to open up the planet. This is the only way for us to be the favorite plush animals on Earth again. You know about the bunnies, don't you? If we manage to attract all kinds of animals, children on Earth will have a variety of toys to choose from. And they will all come from us!"

"What are you saying, Bearmouse? This is the bear planet. Not the planet of all animals!"

"Not yet, President, not yet."

"Well, I think they are all set now. Come on, Knight, let's prepare for the Competition. Please leave us to our work now." Adelaide told the other animals. And the Famous Wood Hound, the Kitchen Giraffe and the Appropriate Horse left the Workshop jumping and laughing. Before they left, the Kitchen Giraffe turned her head and hoped for a quick glance at the Knight's eyes, but he did not turn around, and his visor was closed.

As she left with the others, the Kitchen Giraffe felt that she had left something behind, and inside she felt a strange little pang. But she did not know why.

"Do you want to go to the Bear Park?" The Wood Hound asked. "You liked the trees there, didn't you?"

Now that the three new animals were fitted with Wish Captors, they shared the memory loss that the bears experienced on the planet, so the Kitchen Giraffe asked:

"Did I? I don't remember."

"Wooof! Oh, we are becoming bears now."

"Weeeheehee! I am not! I am not losing my memory! Weeheeheee! I am the Appropriate Horse of the Knight of the Round Ear!"

"You are very lucky, you see. I have this strange feeling inside me, and I don't know what it is."

"Wooof! Come on, Kitchen Giraffe, let's go to the Bear Park! It is a perfect, happy place!"

"Come on? I think someone else has said that to me before, you see."

And they were off to the Bear Park.

The Kitchen Giraffe cries holes in the ground

Nanuk was still wandering about in the Bear Park although no new bear had appeared like that, as Bearmouse had promised in his show. Nanuk was turning into a teddy bear more and more, losing his Earth polar bear size and growing smaller and softer with every polar teddy bear wish that landed on his Wish Captor. He was losing all hope that he would witness a spontaneous bear creation. Now, when he looked at the note reminding him that bears might appear in the Bear Park out of the blue, he did not even really understand what it said. He started to lose the memory of the memory itself, but it was time for a new Bearmouse show very soon and Nanuk would be able to refresh his knowledge.

When the Famous Wood Hound, the Appropriate Horse and the Kitchen Giraffe reached the trees in the Bear Park, the Kitchen Giraffe began to cry. No one on the planet of the bears had ever cried before, and no one bearing a

Wish Captor had ever cried before either. The planet was founded on the fact that losing track of events makes the mind carefree and therefore it was impossible for the bears to feel sad, as they would not know why they were sad. But the Kitchen Giraffe had slipped back into possibilities for a while and had encountered a new emotion there. She did not understand what this emotion was, but she knew that it had taken hold of her whole being, and not knowing why made her cry.

Last time sadness got a hold of the Giraffe, she fell into Imagination. But now, she had a Wish Captor and was a fully accepted imaginary creature. She had moved out of the possibilities and had the right to exist on an actual planet, she was not as fragile anymore.

Yet still, something bothered her very much but she did not understand what it was. And it made her cry.

"What's the matter with you, Kitchen Giraffe?" asked the Appropriate Horse.

A big tear rolled down her nose. When it touched the tip, it mixed with the remaining trace of Magic Potion that had stayed there since her nose had touched the bottle. And when the tear and the Magic Potion drop fell to the ground together, a hole appeared in the reality of the planet.

"Wooof! What did you do? Stop crying, please," said the Wood Hound. But it was too late. The Kitchen Giraffe's sadness had started to upset the reality of the planet, and would soon be spreading to the parallel worlds.

"Wheeeheeeheee! You made a hole in the ground! How did you do that?"

"I don't know!" The Kitchen Giraffe, becoming alarmed, cried some more. And every time a tear fell to the ground, another hole formed.

The Famous Wood Hound sniffed at the hole, but his nose was immediately sucked into the void. He withdrew it quickly.

"Hey, maybe I should quickly travel to the Forest of the Same Name, perhaps my pies could help!"

On Earth, a child looked at his bear and said "Oh no, he is not a bear anymore, this is unbearable!"

Adelaide was about to check all the Wish Captors on her screens when she noticed a total malfunction. The screwdriver was knocking at the screens, trying to unscrew some parts but was unable to succeed. Bearmouse said "Squeak!" and did not know what to do either.

"You see what happens when other animals are allowed on the planet," Teddy Bear said, and paced angrily around the workshop.

"What is going on here? Knight of the Round Ear! Help!"

"I need my Appropriate Horse for that. And Hazelnut should be here!"

Hazelnut was supervising the observation session and looked at the blinking Wish Captors on all the bears. The telescopes did not show anything, and the whole universe seemed to be upside down.

"What's going on?" A bear asked, his muzzle had moved to the backside of his head. His voice was muffled.

"I don't know. The properties are malfunctioning," said Hazelnut, noticing that his own ears had moved strangely away from their usual place.

Faufur interrupted his bear language lesson and ran to the Bear Park. He had to take care of the Magic Potions in case something threatened the balance of the parallel worlds. He passed by the new animals and tried to find a bottle of Magic Potion in a tree. "Quickly! I need to restore the properties to their right place." The animals looked at him in bewilderment.

"What's going on?" they said, almost at the same time.

"The Magic Potion! Did any of you touch it?" Faufur asked.

"I might have, you see," the Kitchen Giraffe said, and blushed with shame. "I don't remember."

"Don't touch it, please. The whole balance of the planet depends on the Magic Potion!" And Faufur picked up the bottle and ran away with it.

"What's going on here?" Nanuk asked. He had trudged to the place where the others had gathered and wondered: "Where are the bears?"

"I think I have caused quite a fuss, you see." The Kitchen Giraffe tried to hide behind a tree. "I suddenly felt so sad."

"Sad?" Nanuk asked. "What is that?"

Faufur ran off to the observation session and hastily poured some Magic Potion over the confused bears. "That should work, at least for now." Faufur mumbled and tried to restore their shapes with a few drops.

"Faufur!" Little Creamy had arrived to the observation session. "The screwdriver has been acting very strangely."

"I don't think it is the screwdriver's fault. Something has upset the universe. The bears are losing their shape!"

"The wishes?"

"No, the wishes are fine. The Kitchen Giraffe touched the Magic Potion."

"Yes, I know. But she did not know what the potion was for. It should not be causing such a distress."

Meanwhile, the Knight of the Round Ear and Adelaide had arrived at the Telescope Park as well.

"I know what to do!" The Knight said. And he told the bears to practice a little for the Nuzzle Competition. And they started doing the Nuzzle with the Muzzle to one another. After a while, the properties rearranged themselves properly, but did not seem very stable.

"We have to get ready. Practice, practice, don't stop."

Faufur poured a little Magic Potion on them. The bears practiced some more. Their Wish Captors calmed down a little.

"What happened in the Imagination, Knight?" Adelaide asked and tried to get a good look at the Knight's eyes. His visor was shut, but he seemed able to see through it just fine. He tried to look through one of the telescopes and check if the bears on Earth were still visible.

"What do you mean?"

"I mean, what happened in the Imagination? How did you find the Kitchen Giraffe?"

"I found her, and I brought her back. Like you asked me to. There is nothing more to it." And the Knight turned a screw on the telescopes, which made the telescope shriek a little. "Hey!"

"What was that?" The Knight cocked his head.

"Don't tickle me!" The telescope said to the screwdriver. The Knight of the Round Ear had picked up Little Creamy's screwdriver in the Workshop without realizing it could translate the telescope's feelings.

"Telescope, is that you?" The Knight ventured.

"Of course, it's me. You tickled me! You bears just don't understand when we talk to you!"

"Well, this has never happened before."

"Has it not?"

"No."

"You wouldn't know anyway. You don't remember anything." The telescope said, and it sounded like it was folding its arms on its chest in disappointment.

Little Creamy came running and stopped in front of the telescope talking to the Knight of the Round Ear. "Have you discovered anything?"

"Well, the telescope is ticklish. Otherwise, nothing." The Knight said.

"The telescope? Did it talk to you?" Creamy said, without really knowing why.

"Yes, it did, actually. How did you know?"

"I don't know."

"Come on, EMOT! You must remember this. I have shown you the other animals."

Obviously, the memory loss did not affect the telescopes.

The Knight of the Round Ear looked at Little Creamy who looked at the screwdriver.

"Let me try something." And Creamy took the screwdriver from the Knight's paw and tried to turn a screw right on top of the telescope's eyepiece.

"Hihihi!" The telescope started giggling.

"Yes, I remember now. The telescope has shown me the Kitchen Giraffe, the Appropriate Horse and the Famous Wood Hound."

The Knight's visor made a little "Clong!" sound when the Kitchen Giraffe was mentioned, but no one noticed.

"Interesting," he said. "The screwdriver makes you remember things."

"And he translates, too. Amazing tool. If only I could remember where I got it from," Creamy said.

Little Creamy scratched his head, put a paw under his chin and said "Mm hmmm" a few times in a row.

"Hugh Bear"

Since he had started receiving the best teddy bears on Earth, Hugh had renamed his toy store "Hugh Bear." He had thought of the name after talking to Faunour. As Faunour sounded French, he thought Hugh Bear would be a fitting name for his shop as it sounded like Hubert in French.

Since Harriet was home for Christmas, Hugh had a little more time to relax. But with the Holiday Season, he had a lot going on at the store and many customers came in who wanted to purchase the perfect bears they had been hearing so much about.

But, as it happened, precisely on that day, he suddenly noticed a change in the appearance of his perfectly shaped teddy bears. Their noses had moved to the side, the ears seemed misplaced. And very quickly, people gathered in his store and started shouting at him, waving bizarrely shaped bears at him, and Hugh did not understand what was happening.

"Look at the bear! Look! What is happening to him?" A mother screamed.

"This is not a perfectly shaped teddy bear! We expect only perfectly shaped bears from you!" A father said, very annoyed.

"Please calm down, people! I don't know what is happening!"

Anton looked down at Nelson, his favorite bear. His nose had moved to the back of his head, and doing the Nuzzle with the Muzzle seemed quite impossible for him now. Anton started sobbing, and Hugh looked at his son, and then at the people in his shop. He took off his glasses, rubbed his eyes, and sighed. He didn't know what to do.

"Don't worry, Daddy," Anton said between two sobs. "I know Faunour and the Knight of the Round Ear will fix this."

"What are you talking about?" Hugh asked his son, still rubbing his eyes.

"You know the bears on the planet Alas-K, the planet of bears."

Hugh looked at his son and had a sudden recollection. Faunour, … "Yes, I remember a bear called Faunour."

"Yes, Faunour is in charge of the teddy bears who arrive on Earth and fall asleep. Mom and Faunour ship them to us, when she is there with him. Perhaps something has gone wrong now that she is with us?"

And then, Hugh suddenly remembered. The teddy bears

he sold in his shop came from another planet. He wondered if he should try and call Faunour.

The children in his bear shop cried and screamed louder and louder. The parents yelled at him. Hugh lost his patience.

"Please, you have to leave now. We will fix this. The bears will be restored, don't worry."

"But look at them! What's wrong with them?" The parents insisted.

"Please, please, let me think. You really need to leave now!"

And he escorted the angry parents with their children out of his shop.

"My bear!" A little girl sniveled while Hugh pushed her gently but decisively towards the door. "Don't worry, the bears are going to be fine."

"Please, Mister Hugh, do something. We can't go on like this."

"I know," Hugh said. "Neither can I" he muttered to himself.

When the last angry customer had finally left his shop, he sat down next to his son and sighed.

"Anton, what are we going to do?"

"Sad?"

In the Bear Park, the Appropriate Horse and Ademar, the Famous Wood Hound tried to comfort the Kitchen Giraffe who was still making holes in reality with her tears. There, another tear rolled down her long neck and landed on a tree root. The root suddenly was cut off the ground where the tear had landed, and there was nothing. A hole with nothing in it.

"Weeeheehee! Look! There is nothing!"

"Woof! Nothing! How can that be? I should go back to my bakery and get some blueberry pie. Reality is not supposed to have holes like that."

"Wait! Look at the Giraffe."

The Kitchen Giraffe was staring in front of her, and sobbed, but she didn't lose any properties this time and did not slip into Imagination. She just stared into the void and cried.

"What's wrong, Kitchen Giraffe? Please tell us."

"I don't know, you see. I have very strange sensations in my stomach. At the same time a terrible pressure on the stomach and then some kind of excitement, as if I had butterflies flying around inside me and I am shaking. I have never felt like this before, you see."

"Butterflies?" Ademar asked.

"Yes, like very light things with wings flying around inside me. Aren't those butterflies?" And she wished for butterflies so hard that there was a whole swarm swirling around them. "You see, butterflies. Like them. They are inside me."

"Do you think it is because of the Wish Captor?" The Horse asked.

"I feel fine with mine. Just had a little itching the first moments but no sensations of butterflies or pressure of any kind. Woof!" said the Famous Wood Hound.

The Appropriate Horse looked at the Wood Hound impatiently.

"Just saying." And he curled up in a corner.

"Well, there must be another reason then."

"My hat is back. Which is good, you see." The Kitchen Giraffe said, before starting to cry again.

"Please, Kitchen Giraffe, please, stop crying! You make holes in reality."

Thanks to the Magic Potion, hidden in the tree hollows, the reality of the planet Alas-K was balanced.

But the Kitchen Giraffe had slipped back into Imagination, and there, everything was possible. It was the world of possibility and wishes, and she had opened herself once more to a possible and different creation. All of her properties were lost instantly, but she had been made whole again when the Knight of the Round Ear recognized her as the Kitchen Giraffe. And yet, something had happened when they were both in the Imagination. A moment had slipped away.

"Woof! I know. The Kitchen Giraffe is *sad!*"

"But, why would she be sad? She has just been saved from Imagination by the Knight of the Round and has safely returned to us."

The Kitchen Giraffe blinked a little when the Knight of the Round Ear was mentioned, and she felt a clear rush of butterflies in her stomach.

"Kitchen Giraffe, are you sad?"

"I don't know, you see. I don't think I have ever experienced this state before. I can't say it is very enjoyable. Or is it? You see, I am not sure. I am confused." And she looked quickly at the tree and turned her head even faster to see if the tree would follow and she turned so quickly that there was no picture of the tree in her mind, just a hole.

"Oh no, you were right. I create holes in reality now. Oh, wait. No, no, this is the way it is supposed to be." The Kitchen Giraffe was very confused.

The Famous Wood Hound whispered to the Appropriate Horse: "Something is very wrong here. Let's go to the Telescope Park and try to find out what they are doing. Perhaps they have found a clue."

"Weeheeehee! Good idea. But can we leave her alone here?"

"Wait. I will ask Nanuk to keep an eye on her." And the Famous Wood Hound trotted away to find Nanuk.

Nanuk was wandering about and muttering to himself. "A bear creation! A spontaneous bear creation! What would that even look like? Why a bear creation? Ah, yes, this is the planet of the bears. What an idea? A planet of bears! Ah, the planet where wishes create bears who become teddy bears on Earth. I should look for the rocket that brought me here, and Robotbear as they call him. Robotbear who does not become a teddy bear when he goes to Earth because he is immune to the Earth atmosphere that transforms Alas-K bears into teddy bears…"

"Hey, Nanuk!" The Famous Wood Hound interrupted Nanuk's muttering.

"Oh, the non-bears again. What's up? And where are the bears, if you don't mind me asking…"

"Nanuk, we are very sorry. We don't know what happened to the spontaneous bear creations, but we need your help."

"Well, I haven't witnessed a bear creation yet, so I suppose I can help non-bears instead." Nanuk seemed quite a bit disappointed, and sighed.

"You know the Kitchen Giraffe, yes? Do you remember her?" The Appropriate Horse remembered that the bears did not have memory and so he tried to trigger some kind of remembrance mechanism by mentioning the Kitchen Giraffe.

"Well, I am not sure. But I understand that she is not a bear. Like you two."

"Yes, indeed. She is not a bear. She is over there and she seems to be sad."

"Sad. This emotion does not exist here on this planet. I am quite sure of it."

"Yes, we know that. But she brought it here anyway. And that's why she is upsetting reality and making holes in it by crying."

"Of course, the Kitchen Giraffe makes holes in reality by crying. Listen to yourselves. You don't make any sense, but why would you? Non-bears don't make sense." Nanuk said and smiled to himself.

The Horse and the Wood Hound exchanged glances, and smiled at Nanuk.

"Of course, you are right. But please, come with us and talk to the Kitchen Giraffe. Meanwhile, we have to go to the Telescope Park and see if they have fixed the reality problem."

"You mean the problem with the holes?"

"Well, the holes are just one aspect of the disturbed reality. I think the bears' properties are confused regarding their locations."

"The bears?" Nanuk seemed suddenly more interested when the conversation revolved around bears again. "Their properties are confused?"

"Yes. It seems like the muzzle moves to the back of the head and the ears move to another place as well."

"Oh? I have not noticed that until now."

And Nanuk checked his nose and his ears. Everything seemed to be in the right place. He also had a look at his Wish Captor. A few more wishes had formed and his stars were brightly colored.

"Oh no, the Wish Captor! I don't remember what it does exactly but something unpleasant is connected to it."

"You lost your head!"

At that moment, a signal called the population to the television room. Bearmouse's show was about to begin. The bears on the planet Alas-K had all forgotten by now that they would one day have to go to Earth and become teddy bears. Everyone that is, except Nanuk who had written down some of the information Bearmouse had given him in his show which triggered a memory thread.

"Squeak!" A voice said very loudly. "Dear all, please come to the television room of the Government Building. We need you all to be present. We need to discuss very urgent issues concerning our reality and our properties. Bears and non-bears alike, please gather immediately."

Bearmouse had found a megaphone and thought it would be useful to summon both the bears and the newly formed non-bears, thereby finally assembling an acceptable number of viewers as his audience.

Teddy Bear strode across Main Street and the other bears

followed him closely to the Government Building. Everyone was anxious to learn about the emergency situation.

The Knight of the Round Ear was still looking at the telescope and the telescope still giggled every time the screwdriver touched it. He opened his visor and looked through the eyepiece. "Look, Creamy! Look at the bears on Earth!"

And Little Creamy looked at the bears on Earth through the eyepiece and saw something very strange.

"Can you see it, too?" The Knight asked.

"Do you mean their properties? The muzzle is on the wrong side of the head…"

"And the ears seem to be moving!"

"Come on." The Knight said. "Let's go watch Bearmouse's show. We need to fix this."

And they both went to the Government Building and joined the group that had already formed in the television broadcasting room.

...

In the Bear Park, Nanuk had found the Kitchen Giraffe.

"Kitchen Giraffe! I was asked to keep an eye on you. What seems to be the problem? I see you still have your lovely hat," Nanuk said to the Kitchen Giraffe, trying to distract her from the reality problem she had caused, and was now trying to resolve by herself.

"Oh, Nanuk. I didn't have the funnel *but then* I found it *again*. I had lost it, but then it was restored to me. Or maybe it was created anew? I don't understand, you see. But here, look. When I turn my head, the tree doesn't follow me right away. It loses time. This is not normal, you see."

The Kitchen Giraffe was very distressed, adding "you see" to her comments even more than usual.

"Just you try it. Look at the tree and turn your head."

Nanuk did as he was told. The picture of the tree very slowly faded in the corner of his eye, and it seemed to take forever to fill up again when he turned his eyes back to the tree.

...

Meanwhile, Bearmouse began his show the way he usually did.

He started his sentences with "Squeak!" and reminded his audience that Alas-K bears have three different origins: they were spontaneously created by wishes, or they could have come from Earth as real life bears, or they were old teddy bears who had been lost or abandoned. The purpose of the Alas-K bear was to become a beautiful teddy bear for a child on Earth in order to comfort him with the Nuzzle with the Muzzle. This information was as usual met with "Ahs" and "Ohs" of surprise, but then, Bearmouse changed the content of his show.

"My dear fellow bears and imaginary creatures. First of all, don't forget that we have no memory.

Right now, something is happening to our planet. As you know, there are newcomers now with us that are not bears, and they have brought new ways of looking at things.

Reality seems to be changing, and even emotions that have never been here before have now made their appearance on the planet.

We need to address this problem by acknowledging that bears might change with this new dimension…"

Teddy Bear cleared his throat, a sign that indicated to the audience, and especially to Bearmouse, that he wanted to speak.

"President, please."

"Bearmouse," Teddy Bear said. "You know how I feel about this new development, however, you and Adelaide have convinced me that the planet should welcome other imaginary animals and creations of the Imagination.

However, as you might probably know, reality is in jeopardy or at least is unsettled by some kind of new emotion that is unheard of here, and the bears, and only the bears, seem to lose their perfect shape. The Knight of the Round Ear has managed to restore some noses by practicing the Nuzzle with the Muzzle. So, please bears, in case your muzzle and ears seem to be on the wrong side of your head, go find Adelaide and she will show you how to practice for the Nuzzle Competition."

On Earth, Faunour had turned on his screen in order to watch Bearmouse's show. He too had noticed that something was wrong with the setting up of the properties, and he was pretty sure that this time it was not his fault. His manipulation of the Wish Captors only had the effect of creating perfectly shaped new animals, not just bears. The new element had not created new animals but confused the shapes of the bears - the teddy bears on Earth and even the live bears catching fish in Alaska. Something terrible must have happened to the bear reality.

Faunour scratched his head, put his paw under his chin and sighed, muttering "mm hmmm" a few times in a row. What could have happened to the bears?

Nanuk tried the game the Kitchen Giraffe had taught him and he found it indeed strange that when he turned his head quickly, the tree became an unrecognizable grey shape, before it formed a nice clear tree picture. When he looked directly at it, it was much clearer than when he turned away, but in-between there was a long pause and even the properties like "green", "brown", "long", "thick" were clearly separated from each other.

"You saw it too, I can tell."

The Kitchen Giraffe had fixed her big eyes on Nanuk and waited for his reaction after he turned his eyes quickly from one side to the other. "What do you think is happening to the properties?"

The children in the Hugh Bear store were crying again although they tried to do the Nuzzle with the Muzzle with bears whose muzzles and ears would not retain a stable shape long enough in order to do the Nuzzle with the Muzzle properly. Without that comfort, the children grew extremely agitated and cried and protested and threw themselves on the floor. Hugh looked at Anton who looked at Nelson. All the bears had suddenly lost their stability as their properties swirled around in a state of indetermination.

Nanuk looked at the Kitchen Giraffe and noticed a tear rolling down her neck. "You are crying," he said.

"Yes, but I don't know why." The Kitchen Giraffe said.

"You said you had lost your head and recovered it."

"I never said any such thing. I said I had lost my hat."

"Oh, did I say "head"? I am sorry."

The Kitchen Giraffe gave Nanuk a look of indignation, but then she realized that he might have an interesting point.

"Why do you think I lost my head?"

"Well, when one loses their hat, they sometimes lose the head that goes with it."

"Do they, now?" The Kitchen Giraffe also found Nanuk a little annoying.

"Do you remember what happened?"

"Well, yes. Teddy Bear insulted me. He said that giraffes don't have stripes. Then I ran out of the workshop and then, I don't remember."

"That's not a lot. And also, very strange. You remember everything that happened on the planet where there is no memory. In the Imagination, on the other hand, there is nothing but memory. You should be able to remember what happened there.

The Kitchen Giraffe tried to force her memory as Nanuk had done when Bearmouse interviewed him.

She blushed a little, and all she could come up with was "Clong!"

"Clong?" Nanuk said.

"Love!"

The Famous Wood Hound and the Appropriate Horse had just missed the Knight of the Round Ear and Little Creamy when they arrived at the Telescope Park. Hazelnut was still there, packing up.

"Hazelnut! Do you know what is going on here?"

"Oh, hello, new animals! I don't think we have been properly introduced."

The Famous Wood Hound and the Appropriate Horse introduced themselves properly and then they asked again: "So, do you know what is going on?"

Hazelnut did not look too friendly, they thought, but they didn't know who else to ask.

"You are talking about the property confusion, I suppose."

"The property confusion? We are talking about the holes."

"The holes?"

"Yes, the Kitchen Giraffe's tears create holes in the reality of the planet."

"They do? That's astonishing!"

"Well, she has her own unique way of perceiving things…"

"I think she must have put her nose into a Magic Potion bottle. The potions keep our reality stable."

The Famous Wood Hound and the Appropriate Horse wondered how Hazelnut managed to remember these things.

"Bearmouse! All the bears have gathered here. Adelaide and I will check their Wish Captors. Come on, bears, form a row and we will see if your Wish Captors are in a good shape."

The Knight of the Round Ear started checking each bear who was standing in line, one by one. The bears had an obvious stability problem and their muzzles and their ears seemed to be moving.

"Do the Nuzzle with the Muzzle the way Adelaide has taught you. Each one of you turn to the bear next in line and do the Nuzzle with the Muzzle."

Again, the practice seemed to be working at least a little, and the properties stabilized themselves.

"So, what do you mean by that?" The Appropriate Horse asked Hazelnut, referring to the Magic Potions.

"Only Faufur and Teddy Bear are allowed to touch the Magic Potion bottles. Usually, they are also the only ones who can see them because they contain the balance between reality and all possibilities. The bear planet was created out of time, so all memory or emotion was banned. In order to become teddy bears, the bears need to be void of feelings and goals of their own. On Alas-K they can neither fear nor love. In the Imagination on the other hand, everything is possible."

The Horse looked at the Hound and the Hound looked at the Horse. "Clong!" They both said in unison, and as they ran off to the government building, they called out,

"Thanks, Hazelnut! You are very knowledgeable!"

....

"Clong?" The Kitchen Giraffe cocked her head. "What is that sound?"

"Come with me, Kitchen Giraffe. I think we are late for the show."

And Nanuk took the Kitchen Giraffe by the hoof. "I need to show you something."

Adelaide watched the Knight of the Round Ear gather the bears, regrouping them, starting the Nuzzle with the Muzzle again and again, from all possible angles. Meanwhile, Faunour had called and reported that the teddy bears had lost their perfect shape as well, and that even Earth bears' shapes were becoming distorted.

While trying to get the bears to recover a perfect shape, his visor dropped a few times, and the Knight of the Round Ear could not see. "Clong!"

The Kitchen Giraffe and Nanuk arrived in front of the government building at about the same time as the Famous

Wood Hound and the Appropriate Horse. They all looked at one another and said "Clong!"

"Why is everybody making this obnoxious sound? I don't understand," the Kitchen Giraffe said. "I need to work on reality a little more."

"No, no, please don't do that! You need to see someone. Come with us."

And they led the Kitchen Giraffe inside the emergency Nuzzle with the Muzzle workshop that was set up in the government building.

"Here!"

And the Kitchen Giraffe looked at the Knight of the Round Ear and then she felt the butterflies and the pressure again, and a tear ran down her face.

"Is he causing this?" She asked, looking at the others and batting her eyelashes.

"We do think so," the animals said. "You should go to him. He has worn this armor for far too long."

"Yes, his armor! I remember now. He didn't want me to fix his visor problem."

"You can do much more than that. You know how to do the Nuzzle with the Muzzle, don't you Kitchen Giraffe?"

"I think so, but is that acceptable here, in front of everyone, you see?"

The animals laughed. "But, Kitchen Giraffe, this is a Nuzzle with the Muzzle Workshop."

"I know that. But there are different kinds of Nuzzle, it seems to me."

"I think you will be fine. Just do it. Our reality can't stand any more holes. Look at the poor bears, they are totally unstable. You must solve this."

"I can fix this? Are you sure?"

"Well, at least you can restore happiness. And that's what the Nuzzle with the Muzzle does."

The Kitchen Giraffe slowly moved toward the Knight of the Round Ear. She had a lot of butterflies flying around in her stomach now and the pressure was practically unbearable.

The Knight of the Round Ear was very busy organizing the bears according to the shape and color of their Wish Captors. The Giraffe came up close to him and tapped him on the shoulder.

"Knight of the Round Ear! I need to do something, you see."

And very slowly she rubbed her nose on his head, and when she started touching his armor with her nose, his helmet began to light up. In fact, the helmet became so bright that all the animals gasped. Then the helmet vanished in the light and for the first time, everyone could see the face of the Knight of the Round Ear. And they could see that he also had stripes on his head. The Giraffe tried again to rub her nose on his cheek but now he could do it himself and he rubbed his straight muzzle on the Giraffe's cheek a few times in a row. And slowly, very slowly his armor opened, his body was freed and the Giraffe took his paw.

"That is an appropriate moment! Wheeeheeeheee!" said the Appropriate Horse.

All the bears applauded, then checked their ears and their muzzles. Every muzzle and every ear was in the right place again.

The reality did not have holes anymore. Nanuk checked, turning his head quickly, back and forth. The picture fragment followed his gaze quickly and now he did not notice a pause anymore.

Faunour called and said "OK, planet Alas-K, everything is fine."

The children in Hugh Bear's shop looked at their bears and saw that their properties were in the right place again: the ears on top of their heads, and the muzzle in the middle of their faces. All the children took their bears and had them jump on their chest and do the Nuzzle with the Muzzle. The children smiled and ran home to play.

A famous band started playing. They called themselves "bearbearbear", and their song "bears will be bears" filled the whole universe.

And this was how love was created on the planet of the bears.

Tigah raised his paw and said "But still, I am quite sure that it was our invention!"